SURESH KOHLI (b. 1947) is a multi-dimensional personality: poet, literary critic, editor, translator, film historian and documentary filmmaker. He has over 30 published works (including a novel) and a hundred literary and cultural short films to his credit. A widely travelled person, his films have been screened in Australia, France, Germany, Spain, Nepal and the UK, apart from India. He lives and works in New Delhi.

An Evening in Paris and Other Stories

Edited by
Suresh Kohli

OM
Om Books International

Published in 2014 by

OM

Om Books International

Corporate & Editorial Office
A-12, Sector 64, Noida 201 301
Uttar Pradesh, India
Phone: +91 120 477 4100
Email: editorial@ombooks.com
Website: www.ombooksinternational.com

Sales Office
4379/4B, Prakash House, Ansari Road
Darya Ganj, New Delhi 110 002, India
Phone: +91 11 2326 3363, 2326 5303
Fax: +91 11 2327 8091
Email: sales@ombooks.com
Website: www.ombooks.com

ISBN: 978-93-83202-16-4

10 9 8 7 6 5 4 3 2 1

Printed in India

Contents

Introduction

The number of short stories Abbas wrote in either Urdu or English, or both, has largely been a matter of conjecture. He was his own editor and translator, and barring a handful of exceptions like 'A Debt to Pay', or 'Sardarji', rendered into English by the late Khushwant Singh as 'The Death of Sheikh Burhruddin', based on a real life incident to which the author had been privy, and indeed the inventive, 'Mansuri 1952' or 'Half a Man', one of the earliest reflections on aspects of movie-making in India, translated by the writer for this volume, almost the entire body of Abbas's work in English had been entirely his own.

The attempt to resurrect most of Abbas's short stories and novellas, with their distinct themes and preoccupations, from available sources is a daunting task, as is also reconstructing the sequence in which they might have been crafted over different periods. That said, cast as simple narratives, the stories and themes do sometimes indicate a period. The language is simple and crisp, and the subjects deal with stark deprivation, want, exploitation, need in pre-Independence India, with reflections on hopes, dreams and aspirations of people influenced by Nehruvian socialism and nation building, highlighting the rural situation to which Mahatma Gandhi sought to draw attention in pre-Independence India, with Jawaharlal Nehru, independent India's first prime minister underscoring the same issue later as well.

Almost all Abbas's early stories deal with starvation, hunger, and the undying human spirit. Propelled by a sense of equality and reason that seemed to manifest itself through the October Revolution, Abbas chased the idea of socialism as a professed goal. An intertextual approach to his oeuvre reveals interesting insights.

Going through Abbas's first published collection, *Rice and Other Stories*, San Francisco-based writer, editor, film enthusiast, Nivedita Ramakrishnan blogs finds it: "a thin volume of ten short stories that can be read in one go. The stories are about ordinary people in ordinary situations—with candid glimpses into life's extraordinary moments. Every now and then, the veil lifts to reveal life's surprises, its splendours, its ironies." She continues: "Reality is what we see on the outside, but it is also what we fleetingly see on the inside, made visible through cracks and gaps. And it is to those cracks and gaps that Abbas draws our attention—although I distinctly felt a certain predictability about Abbas's style, which kind of dampens the reader's attention. The same does not hold true of his films, which are vastly more imaginative. Halfway through many of the stories, I correctly guessed what the ending would be! For me, maudlin is the word that describes the treatment of many of the stories.

"The title story, 'Rice', is about Durga, a poor mill worker's wife who delivers her baby when she is out, standing in the long queue to buy rations. It is stark and grim, and yet represents the joys of new beginnings.

The queue is relentless, but hungry mouths have to be fed, and hundreds of women patiently wait their turn outside the government grain store, miraculously open after many days, during a period of grain shortage (which is reminiscent of the darkness of the Bengal Famine of 1943, captured on celluloid in *Dharti ke Lal* [1946]). Crowds teem around and bags are filled with rice; birth—at once mundane and magical—unfolds."

On the prickly issue of which story was written when, why and how, was 'The Gun', dedicated to the late actor, Smita Patil, and which appears in the 1985 collection *The Gun and Other Stories* written first or 'Rice' that had been included as the title story in his first compilation in 1947? Or was it 'Thicker Than Water', for that matter? All three are set in rural India, in the early phase of post-Independence India in what Nehru called the new temples. Caste, unemployment, discrimination based on religion were some of the other concerns. It was not merely an attempt to capture, as some critics had suggested, "the wide chasm that exists between the rich and the poor in India." Abbas had himself witnessed these during his travels, as elaborated upon in his autobiography.

'Father and Sons', one of his critic's points out "depicts protest as an eternal necessity for change and progress" and seeks to demonstrate the expected transition from feudalism to democratic norms. To a lesser degree, this is also evident in 'The Gun'. Interestingly the landscape is part of the narrative: "Walking through the village, he (Ruldoo Ram) arrived in Harijanwadi where the lanes were unpaved, where the gutter of dirty waters flowed in the middle of the 'road', where there was mud and filth everywhere, where worms wriggled in the puddles of dirty water, and where the well was also *kaccha*."

'Rice' begins thus: "Twisting like a serpent, creeping at a snail's pace, buzzing like a swarm of bees, two long queues—one of men, the other of women—were advancing towards the government's grain shop. The women's queue was even longer than the men's—quite a furlong in length, with its tail end in a narrow alley round the street corner."

A number of Abbas's works deal with working in front and behind the curtains of Hindi cinema during his times. In depicting reality, he does not shy away from commenting on the seamy side of the glamour world. 'Saturday Night Fever' deals with the trials and tribulations of an aspiring young female actor: "Several so-called producers had 'interviewed' her, approved of her good looks, declared her to be photogenic, taken her out for drinks dinners and dances. She had thought that the high road to film fame and fortune lay through the hotel rooms of the 'producers'. She had taken the plunge, been tested and tasted by a whole range of 'producers' and directors but the only thing she got out of that was 'I was a maiden once!'"

The grime behind the glamour has also been a recurrent concern in the experimental 'Half a Man' that otherwise is a narrative that unfolds that through a series of letters a young woman writes to another, also seeking to show the dismal face of success—illusory and real as the same time. He also partially returns to comparisons between reality and myopic illusions in 'The Physiotherapist'.

'The Naked Fakir', also made into a short film (the present writer applied greasepaint, playing one of the murderers), deals with a man whose religion is compassion. Fearing danger to their religion in his presence, a Christian priest, a Hindu *pandit* and a Muslim *maulvi* provoke Michael, Ramu and Masita, to kill him. The killing having been carried out, when they lift the blanket, there is no sign of the fakir, played by Pankaj Kapoor.

Although Abbas repeatedly emphasised his commitment to mankind through various forums, he enlisted this as one of his manifestos in his autobiography, *I Am Not An Island:* "I still (at the age of sixty-two, after a paralytic attack) feel alive and involved in mankind. I still admire a beautiful face—though I can only see it when it comes within kissable range. I still feel enthusiastic about certain causes—freedom, socialism and peace, among them. I am *alive*. But I am prepared for death, which may come today or (hopefully) after 20 years! I hope it will come (whenever it comes) when I will still be writing the last page for my friend Russi Karanjia of *Blitz*. In fact, the 'Last Page', I hope, shall be published as a posthumous document. Indeed, if there is life after death (about which I am still subject to scepticism), I will be glad to send despatches from the other world."

Unlike his friends and contemporaries in the Progressive Writers' Movement, Abbas almost never seems to have wavered in his professed goal of concentrating on the positive, even in situations of despair. His stories are based on observed reality, and not merely imagined. In my youthful exuberance, and, perhaps, while attempting to arrive at my own conclusion on the matter, I asked him to explain the difference between the perceived and the observed, the real and imagined. He said, "The difference between realism and social realism is that unlike the former, in the latter case, the author is involved and feels—he expresses his rational anger and a sense of indignation and he expresses his desire that the injustice be ended."

This was the leitmotif of all his creative expressions.

At a time when many more raconteurs of short fiction, especially in Urdu and Hindi, had stolen the thunder from amongst those involved in the Progressive Writers' Movement, Abbas often wrote different and innovative stuff. And not necessarily for the wrong reasons, one of them being that Abbas did not adhere to or focus on the form itself. While sometimes it cut both ways, the theme or subject being strong, it directed the narrative flow itself. And there were also moments when the narrator in him allowed the intensity of the subject to be overtaken by the situation itself.

What were the larger issues and parameters for Abbas? This third attempt by this writer has been akin to churning the wide, wild ocean anew. One of the reasons could have been that he wrote or rewrote, even over wrote at times, to sustain himself. Money, or the lack of it, was a driving factor, as was the case for Krishan Chander, the most prolific of them all, with the uncanny knack of finding a narrative where, at least for others, non existed. Loneliness could have been another factor in later years that prompted this indulgence.

Another oddity or paradox is that Abbas occasionally changed the title of the same narrative while transferring it from one platform to another. The infamous 'Sardarji', as explained earlier, is a case in point—it was named and renamed time and again. It has appeared under different titles in Urdu, Hindi and English; in the event that it has been rendered in other languages as well, chances are that it would have been rechristened several times. For some strange reason, most of Abbas's fictional have been found their way into, of all the Indian languages, Malayalam.

There is also the queer case of his short stories appearing in one of the two primary languages he had chosen for his creative expression. So it is almost impossible to arrive at an exact number of short stories that he authored during the period that spanned, like for many of his peers, contemporaries and juniors, almost seven decades.

Abbas's very first famous short story 'Ababeel' or 'Sparrows' was supposedly written when he was barely 14. The now defunct *The Illustrated Weekly of India* under Pritish Nandy's stewardship, posthumously published 'Mother and Child', naming it as his last. Considering it deals with the Bhopal gas tragedy, one can only doubt the veracity of the claim, and not really question it, even though the author had been too sick, yet too preoccupied with the completion of his last film under production to have indulged in nostalgia. So for all referential purposes, 'Mother and Child' will go down in literary history as his last go at short literary fiction.

As part of my Introduction to the first volume, *An Evening in Lucknow,* I had sought to provide reasons for what is now turning out to be a Herculean task. I am tempted to reassert, in the third exercise in that direction, the previous hope and belief that some new scholars and critics shall be more ambitious about unearthing the otherwise lost treasure that might provide greater insight into what the author had been trying to convey about India through his shorter fiction. Unfortunately, most of his books are not only out of print, but have also mysteriously disappeared from the shelves of libraries, at least at home. Sadly, the odd critical or analytical work is not very helpful either.

I reaffirm what I wrote while introducing *An Evening in Lucknow* as well as *Sardarji and Other Stories*: "This attempt at resurrecting his forgotten short fiction is in gratitude to his benevolence that one received in plenty. No specific yardstick has been deployed in once again bringing alive these humane stories, encompassing hopes, aspirations, emotions and concerns, desired for any civil society."

In conclusion, I quote Abbas from his autobiography: "My stories in the sanctified field of literature and even in the rarefied field of cinema, have been described, and dismissed, as only the projections of my journalism. Literary critics and film critics jot down the word 'journalese' (which one of them spelt as 'journaleese' obviously to rhyme with cheese!) even before they have had time to read my book or see my film."

Suresh Kohli
June 2014

The Maharaja's Elephant

Once upon a time—and it seems it was very, very long ago, when maharajas were maharajas and not amusing mascots for airlines—the importance of a ruler was reckoned by the number of guns to which he was entitled in a royal salute, the population of his harem, and by the number of elephants in his *feelkhana* (elephant stable).Judged from this standard, Raja Suryakumar Chandra Kumar Vijaysingh Shumsher Jung of Chhamchhampur (only two crackers, seven wives and one elephant) was not among the top 10 or even top 200 of the rulers of princely states. Indeed, his state (area: 1,704 square miles, population: 2,74,589), nestling insignificantly somewhere in the barren plateaus of Central India, was no bigger than a big *zamindari* (of landed gentry) estate, but nevertheless, its relations with the *angrezi sarkar* (British Government) were governed by the terms of a treaty the great-grandfather of the present ruler, the redoubtable Raja Narsinghrao Bimsingh Arjunsingh, had personally signed with Lord Canning.

As a matter of historical record, let it be stated that Chhamchhampur was not always so small and insignificant a state. There was a time when the writ of the Maharaja of Chhamchhampur ran over a great part of Rajputana and what is now known as Madhya Pradesh. But the successive Maharaja's over-fondness for wine (extracted from the *mahua* flowers that grew wild all over the state) and women (especially dancing girls, the chham-chham sound of whose anklet bells was reputed to be the genesis of the state's name: Chhamchhampur) had wreaked havoc with the martial qualities of the ruling family, and one after another, various parts of the state had been swallowed up by the more energetic and avaricious rulers of the neighbouring states, not to mention the big slice that been conceded to the *firangis* (foreigners) in return for the protection afforded by their troops against Chhamchhampur's marauding neighbours.

And thus it had come to pass that by the year 1945, the Maharaja of Chhamchhampur was left only with seven wives and one elephant, and when, under pressure of public opinion, the Viceroy ordered a further cut in the privy purse, the Maharaja found himself financially incapable of maintaining even such a depleted harem and *feelkhana*.

A man of ample girth, nevertheless, he decided to tighten his belt both literally and figuratively. He put all his wives (except the juniormost who was naturally his favourite) on short rations, ordered a cut in their allowances and, on the pretext that robbers were rampant in the state capital, he divested them of their jewels which were duly deposited in the royal treasury for safekeeping, or so it was given out while the fact was that the precious stones were taken out and sent to a firm of jewellers in Bombay, and the gold was melted and secretly sold to a bullion merchant in Delhi. Looking about for further economies, the Maharaja spotted Lakshmi, the solitary old cow elephant in the huge *feelkhana* that was originally designed to house a dozen elephants. According to the Comptroller of the Royal Household, the maintenance of the *feelkhana*, including the rations for the elephant and salary for the mahout, came to no less than Rs. 350 per month, i.e., over 4,000 per year! To the Maharaja's newly awakened sense of economy, this seemed a waste, even for state processions, and the very idea of sitting cross-legged in an uncomfortable howdah struck him as ridiculous when he had a whole fleet of Daimlers and Packards for luxurious driving. So he decided to get rid of old Lakshmi. But he could not afford to lose face by making it public that he was closing down his *feelkhana* because he could no longer afford it. It had to be done with diplomatic circumspection and royal finesse. He was debating the issue in his mind when the Resident, Sir John Rollingston (pronounced Rawlington) was announced.

Sir John was an officer of the Political Department who had risen from the ranks, as it were. The son of a Manchester tailor, he had worked his way through college with the help of scholarships, crammed Latin and Ancient History to get into the Indian Civil Service, and had served for 20 years in various malarious mofussil towns, first as Joint Magistrate and them as Collector, before he was drafted for the Political Department. A secret romanticist who spent all the leisure hours of his bachelor life reading Kipling and Churchill and Yeats-Brown, his original inferiority complex had been transformed into a fascination for what he regarded as the chivalry and old-world charm of India's princely courts. As such, he was more interested in preserving the traditional pomp, pageantry and ceremonies of the princely courts to which he was accredited, than in such prosaic matters as the administration of justice and the improvement of the irrigation system for the benefit of the impoverished peasantry. No wonder Sir John Rollingston (pronounced Rawlington) was held in such affection and esteem by the princes he had served, particularly by the Maharaja of Chhamchhampur.

And so it was natural that in recognition of his services, the Resident should receive a present from the Maharaja and what present could be more appropriate for the romantic soul of Sir John Rollingston (pronounced Rawlington) than a royal elephant, the symbol and epitome of all that pomp and pageantry, chivalry and gallantry that the Manchester tailor's son had always associated with his mission in the princely states of India. And so he was duly grateful for the royal present, and felt greatly moved when the elephant and mahout arrived to take their new quarters in the compound of his bungalow. It seemed to him the crowning moment of his career in India.

But he had not yet reckoned with the economic problem of maintaining an elephant. The few thousands he had been able to put in his bank account were soon gone into the building of an over-sized stable for the elephant. The royal beast had a royal appetite and soon a good bit of the Resident's far-from-ample salary was going into the purchase of sugarcane and other costly rations. The Political Department flatly refused to finance this elephantine adventure and made it clear that the Resident should regard himself lucky if he was not hauled up for so openly accepting a present from the Maharaja—which could easily be construed as illegal gratification. All this was mortifying to the sensitive soul of one who regarded himself as the heir to the Kipling tradition. But with characteristic British tenacity, Sir John Rollingston (pronounced Rawlington) stuck loyally to the elephant, even if it meant his resignation from the club (as he could no longer pay for his whisky-soda bills), giving up the summer vacation in the hills, and other such self-imposed economies. But as every evening he strolled over to the stable, which he liked to call his *feelkhana*, he derived immense consolation from the thought that soon, when he retired, he would take the elephant with him to England where it would lend unparalleled distinction to his semi-detached cottage in Sunningdale or some such place. "That," he would be able to tell his neighbours, "is old Lakshmi, the royal elephant that my friend, the Maharaja of Chhamchhampur, gave me as a present"—and it was a pleasant thrill to anticipate the look of envious wonderment it would produce on the faces of those who had never ventured to the fabulous and exotic lands "East of Suez".

But when the time came for his retirement and impending departure for England, Sir John was dismayed to learn of the immense cost of transporting his royal elephant to England—the train to Bombay and the ship's freight to London amounting to more than the total gratuity to which the retiring civilian was entitled after 25 years in the service of the Empire. He could expect little help or understanding from the bunch of ex-seditionists who had persuaded Whitehall to transfer the Government of India to them, the Maharaja of Chhamchhampur along with many other rulers had agreed to the merger and integration of the state, and it seemed to Sir John Rollingston (no longer pronounced Rawlington but even rudely spelt "Rollingstone" by the raw young Indian officials who had taken over the Secretariat) that the end of the world had come simultaneously with the loss of the brightest jewel in the British crown.

And so, with a heavy heart, he bid goodbye to Lakshmi and by a regular deed—the last document he would sign in India—gifted the elephant to Ganga Ram, the old hereditary mahout who was no less bewildered by the new developments than "Raalingam Saab" as he called the Resident.

With seven *salaams* (salutations) and many low bows of gratitude, Ganga Ram accepted the gift but hardly had his old master's train steamed out of Chhamchhampur Station that the poor mahout was obliged to revise his estimate of this good fortune that he thought had befallen him in acquiring the royal elephant as his personal property. For he was served with a notice to quit the stable along with his *haathi*, as the Resident's bungalow and all its out-houses were being converted by the new administration into a school. With a petition drafted for him by a professional scribe for a fee of two rupees, he went round all the offices but found no sympathy from the new officials. So poor Ganga Ram, suddenly rendered not only homeless but friendless and unwanted in the strange and incomprehensible new world which had risen round him, sat on the neck of old Lakshmi and led her by gentle proddings of his *ankush*, hook used by mahouts, to his village, where their arrival was heralded by much merriment by the village children.

It was his practical-minded wife, however, whose sharp tongue rudely made him aware of the economic crisis he had brought upon himself by accepting such a gift. Not only had they no place to accommodate the gigantic beast in their mud hut, but the produce from their little piece of land (which an earlier Maharaja had given to Ganga Ram's father) was quite inadequate to feed their family, not to speak of the elephant, which would eat more than a dozen human beings put together.

"Give it away to the temple on the hill—a gift to the gods," advised the Old Man of the village, and Ganga Ram, having exhausted his life's savings in feeding the animal just for three days, readily agreed.

With great ceremony, beating of drums and blowing of conches, prayers and intoning of holy mantras, the elephant was accepted by the *pujaris* and *pandits* (priests) of the temple, who felt greatly exhilarated by the gift which proved—or so they thought—that faith was still very much alive, if a poor man like Ganga Ram could bring such a royal gift to the goddess.

To celebrate the occasion, the image of the goddess was placed on the back of the elephant and taken in a procession round the surrounding villages, followed by a crowd mostly of children, drawn less by devotion of faith and more by impish curiosity about an elephant.

But soon the *pujaris* of the temple also learnt the disturbing facts and figures of the royal appetite of the Maharaja's elephant. Since the people in the villages began migrating to the city to work in mills and schools began to lure simple-minded peasants away from the path of faith (or so the *pujaris* thought), the income of the temple from offerings and donations had been steadily dwindling, with the result that now if the elephant had to be fed, the *pujaris* had to starve.

"Then let the beast starve," cried a young hothead among the *pujaris*. "If we keep her a little longer, we will all die of hunger."

The Head Priest advised caution, "Don't forget what the elephant is to the goddess, so we cannot allow her to starve. Moreover, the elephant, too, is a god—the incarnation of our Lord Ganapati of the elephant's head. We will be earning the displeasure of the gods if we ill-treat this noble beast."

"Then you do want us to starve in order to feed this precious elephant?"

"No," the Head Priest calmly went on, "I only wish that this noble animal, this gift to the goddess, this incarnation of our Lord Ganapati, be now gifted to the nation, to serve the people and to be served by them. Of course, that will also save us all from starvation, but that is only incidental."

And so it came to be that on the auspicious day of August 15, old Lakshmi was decorated with sandalwood paste and vermilion and taken to the office of the local Community Project and offered as a gift in the service of the people. Now it can be seen in a certain obscure corner of the country, busy with such humble chores as carrying loads of stone or cement or dragging a gigantic stone roller to level the road.

Which may appear to some like our old friend, Sir John Rollingston (pronounced Rawlington), as a sad come-down for a Maharaja's elephant but there are others, and mahout Ganga Ram (who has been engaged again to look after Lakshmi) is one of them, who say that old Lakshmi has never looked happier in her whole life.

The Prince And The Showgirl

In a pink neon sign above the Shangrila, Bombay's newest night club, the words seemed to blink—and wink!—at the passersby in the street: "Mlle. Fifi from Folies Bergère."

Inside, before her dressing table, sat a diminutive blonde adjusting her golden curls and ringlets. With elaborate ceremony, she pencilled the thin crescents of her plucked eyebrows.

Then, with dainty pincers, she picked up one by one, what looked like a pair of black and hairy centipedes but were really artificial eyelashes, and which she deftly stuck to the rim of the eyelids, thereby doubling the length of the originals.

She proceeded with the ritual with clockwork precision. The face which was shining with greasepaint now received dabs from the powder puff. Then the rough brush went into action and soon the cheeks were glowing red like ripe, red apples. Finally, the lipstick went to work and transformed the thin and somewhat bloodless lips into two thick streaks of the pearly pink shade, which was the latest vogue in the kiss-proof cosmetics. With the touch of the soft make-up pencil, a big, thick black mole appeared on the left cheek. She sniffed the stale air of the ill-ventilated dressing room, closed in from all sides like a prison cell, and immediately reached out for the eau-de-cologne sprayer. The minute particles of the perfumed water glistened against the light, catching different colours of the spectrum like a luminous sunset cloud. This miracle of the cologne spray, a nightly phenomenon, never failed to fascinate her.

From the corridor outside came the muffled sound of the band already playing the overture for her dance number. She got up to have a final look at herself in the mirror, adjusted the belt of the frock with the plunging neck-line, gave a pat to the blonde curls, and let her silk-stockinged feet slip into pencil-point high-heeled shoes which gave her slim body a tantalising arch but made dancing so difficult—and even dangerous—for her.

She opened the door of the dressing room and through the corridor she saw the lights beginning to dim in the hall as the band drummed out a tattoo of suspense to herald her appearance. But before she went out, she rushed to the window for the nightly ritual of one final look at the array of cars parked outside the club, which never failed to thrill her. All these big and rich people, millionaires and even billionaires, she thought with a warm glow of satisfaction, are here to see me. Me, Mlle. Fifi from Folies Bergère, as so colourfully spelt out in the neon sign! But today as she looked out, she saw the most wonderful, sleekest and shiniest sports car being parked. The next moment, the owner of the car had banged the door and rushed into the club, in such a hurry, no doubt, to see her number "Evening in Paris" which had been so well advertised in that evening's papers. As he passed her window, she caught a glimpse of a strong, masculine profile, an athletic body, slim waist and broad shoulders. Her heart missed a beat. Could this be the "Prince Charming" of her dreams? She excitedly ran out of the room and groped her way to her place in the centre of the circular dance floor just as the lights faded in and there was a burst of applause.

"A real Parisian, eh?"

"So chic and cute!"

"I think I saw her in Folies Bergère when I was last in Paris."

"Shh—shh—shh!"

But unlike other days, she listened to these remarks only mechanically, without the tingling sensation which she usually felt when she heard herself being talked about in such flattering terms. Today, not only her eyes but her entire attention was focused on the corner where the owner of the sports car ran, the athletic young man in a form-fitting white Jodhpur coat, smoking a cigarette with what seemed to be a princely air of condescending indifference.

The regular habitués of Shangrila agreed that that night Mademoiselle Fifi excelled herself. In turns, she was the helpless waif, the delectable *demi-mondaine* and the sinister apache, jaunty cap on her blonde head and a cigarette dangling from her nearly pink mouth. She walked on her high heels with a hip-swaying rhythm, she gyrated and pirouetted, and towards the climax of the number, she danced with such gay and characteristically Parisian abandon that everyone clapped and cheered and banged the tables in an unprecedented demonstration of adulation. And after three encores, when the lights finally faded out on her, she had the supreme satisfaction of seeing that he, the nameless "Prince Charming", was as vociferously applauding her as the rest of them.

Sweating with the strain and excitement of the dance, which well nigh exhausted her night after night, she ran into her dressing room, banged the door shut, fell on the sofa and closed her eyes for a few moments of relaxation and the sweet savouring of success. There was a knock on the door.

"Memsaheb," a uniformed waiter was holding a card in his hand, "this Saheb wants to see you."

She snatched the card from the servant's hand, and read the name engraved on it. "Prince Shamshersingh of Sangrampur." Could it be him? Him? Could it be?

She asked the waiter to send the gentleman in, then quickly ran to the dressing table to repair her make-up. She picked up the sprayer and it was through the perfumed rainbow haze of the eau-de-cologne spray that she saw him enter. Yes, it was him.

"Peeleeze seeth thown, Preence," she pouted with the soft 't's' of her French accent, "I am sure very gilad tu see you. You like leetle beet my thanes?"

The Prince, with disarming candour, assured her that he was enchanted by her dancing. "To see you was just like being in Paris. Ah, I love Paris! Tell me, are you Paris-born or from the provinces?"

"I am borned of Paree proper. I am Mademoiselle Fifi from Folies Bergèr," she answered with conviction, pouting a complaint, "You no think I am from gay Paree, Preence?"

"Of course, of course," he assured her, "You look every inch a Parisian. Where do you live—in Montmarte, Montparnasse, or maybe on the Left Bank?"

"No, no, no bank, Monsieur Preence, I pore gal keep monnee in my stocking. You want see? My stocking. You want see? Ha, Ha, Ha." And she laughed. "Tell Fifi about yourself, where your keengtham is?"

Now it was the Prince's turn to laugh, "Kingdom? Oh, no, Sangrampur is just a little state."

"For leetle pore girl like Fifi, you are beeg keeng, Preence!"

"Please don't call me Prince—I really don't deserve the title—we are a republic now, you know..."

"Fifi know very leetle...but I like your kontry and I like you, Preence."

"Really, Fifi. Would you like to live here in India?"

"Yes, Preence."

"And you won't pine for the boulevards of your beautiful Paris?"

"No."

"The sunset on the Place Pigalle?"

"Whath place you speek off?"

"The vast concourse of revellers on July 14, around Les Invalides."

"There are no invalids in my family; my father has asthma but my mother is as strong as a horse."

"Oh, Fifi, you can speak English so well—where did you learn it? Did you go to the Sorbonne?"

"No, I went to St. Joseph's Convent in Byculla...and don't keep on asking me about Paris. Please leave me and go." And she burst into tears.

"But, Fifi, listen—"

"I'm no Fifi—and I'm not from Folies Bergère. I am a girl from Byculla—don't look at me so. All right, I'm a fraud. So what? I do it for a living. But you have no right to come and make fun of me and show me up with all those fancy names. You are a Prince with lots of money to burn up in Paris. So go there, you hear me? But get out from here."

She pushed the protesting Prince out of the room, banged and bolted the room and, flinging the blonde wig from her head, she revealed a mass of curly black hair. Then she abandoned herself to a fit of tears.

An hour later, she got down from a taxi before a ramshackle building in Byculla, groped her way to the fourth floor, climbing the dark and foul-smelling stairs, but as she was about to use her latch-key, she found that the door was open and there was light in the little cubicle which served as their living room.

He was sitting there in one of the ancient sofa chairs with its broken springs and threadbare tapestry.

"What are you doing here?" she could not keep the anger or the tears out of her voice. "We may be poor but we are respectable people. You have no right to come barging in at this hour, even if you are a Prince." "Now listen to me, Fifi—"

"Don't keep calling me Fifi. In my house I'm Joan—"

"And you don't keep on calling me 'Prince'. I'm Johnny."

"Johnny what?"

"Johnny Ferreira. I've already introduced myself to your daddy. He knows my old man."

"But you said you were a Prince."

"I never said it—I only sent my master's card."

"Your master's card. What do you mean?"

"I drive the Prince's car."

"So you are only a chauffeur."

"That's right."

"Then how did you know all that about Paris?"

"I read it in some tourist pamphlets my master brought back from France."

"So you are a fraud?" she spoke through clenched teeth.

But he answered with a smile, "Yes, I, too, am a fraud."

"You mean me," she snapped back, "but I do it for a living, to support my family. Why did you do it?"

"Because it seemed the only way to meet you."

"But why did you want to meet me?" she asked, knowing the answer already.

He walked up to her silently, looked steadily into her eyes, put his hands on her shoulders, then whispered, "Couldn't you guess it, Joan? I had to see you because I love you, have been in love with you—" Then he stopped abruptly.

"Since when?" There was a faint glint of suspicion in her eyes.

"For a long, long time, Joan—but I admired you only from afar."

"Then you know I was not really Fifi from Folies Bergère?"

"Yes, well, you see..."

"And still you put up that act? Really, how mean of you!"

"Well, you see, Joan," and as he spoke she could feel his breath on her cheeks, "there was no other way to bring you back from Paris..."

"Bring me back from Paris? Why do you keep on rubbing that in? You know very well I have never been beyond Apollo Bunder."

"Well, Joan, it is like this. There was no other way of bringing you back from the illusion of Paris to the reality of Byculla."

Through her tears, she whispered, "You are right, Johnny. And I'm glad you brought me back. Keep me here. Don't let me go back, will you?"

And she dissolved into his embrace, which was warm and strong, holding within it the promise and eternity of love and tender protection.

One the third day of their honeymoon, arm in arm, as they strolled past the Shangrila, they looked up and saw the "Fifi from Folies Bergère" neon sign being taken down and a new one being put up in its place. It read: "Dancing Tonight: Señorita Sonia from Spain."

Wheat And Roses

USHA

The sun, the blazing, blinding sun. The scorching look that blew in dusty gusts across the far-flung farm.The deep, oppressive, all pervading silence of the midsummer afternoon, which was only accentuated by the distant dull rumble of a tractor engine.

What a life! thought Usha as she fanned herself with the illustrated film magazine that she had been reading. Fifty miles from the nearest town, this two-room cottage on the farm—a tiny island in the midst of an ocean of billowing wheat fields! No amenities, no comforts. No electric lights, no electric fans, no refrigerator. Even ice was unobtainable. No cinema. The only diversion was provided by a battery radio-set on which she could tune in to Radio Ceylon for a programme of popular film songs. But even this wretched thing broke down every now and then. This time the battery had run down She would have a real quarrel with Ramesh today if he returned from town without the battery, duly charged.

Ramesh! Her husband! Three years they had been married—but, meanwhile, so many changes had taken place in their life that it seemed like ages. Sometimes she felt that the Ramesh she had met in Nainital, with whom she had fallen in love and then married, was a different person altogether and that Ramesh, the Director of the Government's Experimental Farm, was a total stranger.

Three years ago, he had returned from the United States with a degree in Agriculture. Tall, with dark, wavy hair, bright black eyes, in his tweed coat and corduroy trousers, he looked really handsome; almost as handsome as Gregory Peck, who was then Usha's favourite Hollywood hero. Everyone in Nainital that summer had their eyes on him. But Ramesh was attracted only by Usha who had done her Intermediate that year from the Isabella Thoburn College in Lucknow. Usha's father was a prominent lawyer of Allahabad. He, too, had approved of Ramesh because even if the boy was from a poor family, he had been to America on a state scholarship, had got a First Class degree, and was eligible for a good government job.

How wonderfully happy was the first year after their marriage! Ramesh had got a good office job in the Agricultural Department of the Uttar Pradesh Government. Five hundred rupees a month. A bungalow to live in. The carefree social life of the Lucknow officialdom and aristocracy. The glitter and gaiety of Hazratganj, the fashionable shops and cafés and cinema houses. Garden parties in the Government House. Invitations to dinner from the highest officials.

In Lucknow, Usha had everything she desired, but most of all, she was proud of her bungalow which she had decorated and furnished with a great deal of painstaking personal interest. In the garden, she had flower-beds planted with the finest varieties available. The memory of that lovely garden still rankled in her heart. Most of all, she missed the rose bushes which she had herself watered and tended and nurtured and pruned with loving care.

She also remembered the day when the first rosebud had blossomed forth, velvety and scarlet-red. How happy she was on that day! Carefully, tenderly, she had plucked it and placed it in water to keep it fresh during the day. And in the evening, just before the time Ramesh returned from his office, Usha lavished even more than her usual fastidious air on her toilette. She put on a rose-pink sari and placed the flower in the bun of her coiled hair. But all her enthusiasm was miserably dampened when Ramesh failed to notice the rosebud in her hair. That moment of disappointment still rankled in her memory.

"Listen..." And she had hoped that one word would be enough to make Ramesh look at her and then the flower was sure to be spotted.

"Yes, what is it?"

"Nothing"

"Why, I thought you were going to say something."

"Then tell me, how do I look today?"

"As always—very beautiful!"

"You don't notice anything about me now. You are completely changed."

"What do you mean?"

In reply, Usha began to sob and spoke in a tearful voice. "You no longer love me—that's what it is."

For a moment, Ramesh was worried by this accusation, but then he smiled. "Have you suddenly gone crazy? Or has some scandal-monger been telling you tales about me? How on earth did you get this idea that I don't love you any longer?"

"Then why don't you take notice of me now? Remember when we first met in Nainital, before our marriage, you used to notice everything about me. Now, you don't even notice the colour of the sari I am wearing or the scent I have used—or the flower in my hair!"

Now, for the first time, Ramesh looked at the bun of her hair and, pretending to smell the flower, kissed it. "Oh, so, it is because of this that I am being rebuked. All right, if you like, I can compose a whole verse about it. In your beautiful black hair, this rose is like the sun peeping out of dark clouds or a flaming bonfire in the jungle on a black winter night."

"Enough of your mocking," Usha said, laughing through her tears, and so happily ended this first "incident" of their married life. But it left in Usha's heart a peculiar sense of uneasiness and dissatisfaction that was dormant and yet ever-present. This dissatisfaction became vocal when Ramesh began to go, after office hours, to the University botanical laboratory to carry on some research and experiments.

"From morning till evening, you work in the office. In the evening, why do you want to waste your time in this research work?" She made no secret of her disapproval.

"Usha, you know I do this office work only because I am obliged to, to earn a living for both of us. Otherwise it has always been my desire to carry on research on various problems connected with our country's agriculture. So I thought, instead of wasting my time in the evenings, I would go and work for a couple of hours in the University laboratory."

"I still don't understand why you must do that," she countered. "Will this research work mean an increase in your pay?"

"No, I am afraid my salary will remain the same. But it is possible that because of my research, there may be a substantial increase in the production of wheat in our country. I want to continue my research into the causes and cures of the various plant diseases and pests that rob our people of millions of tons of food grains."

"So you think you are doing a great patriotic duty!" she sneered. "But I ask: what has the country and government done for you that you should want to give your life for them? Such a big degree you got from America, and still they pay you only Rs. 500." A part of Usha's dissatisfaction was the permanent grouse as to why her husband's pay was not 1,000 or 1,500 per month.

"Who told you I got such a big degree from America?" Ramesh had an amused smile as he talked very amiably, hoping to convince her by the logic of facts. "If you ask me for the truth, I wasted my time for two complete years. You see conditions—both physical and mechanical—are so different over there that education in the American techniques of agriculture is of no practical value to us. Moreover, Rs. 500 a month is not an amount to be despised. It is more than what millions of our countrymen are able to get. The only grouse I have is that I have been turned into a glorified clerk in the Secretariat, and I have not been given a chance to do some practical work."

She was now more disappointed than angry. "That means that every evening you should go from the office straight to the laboratory and I should sit moping at home, waiting for you, going neither to the club nor to a cinema show nor to a dinner with my friends..."

"Who says you should sit at home all the time. You can go where you like—to the club or your friends, or go with them to the cinema." He tried to cover up his annoyance with a smile.

From that day, they began to spend their evenings separately. Ramesh went straight from the office to the University, and Usha whiled away her time by going to see some film. When they met at dinner, Ramesh would say, "I can't understand how you can see a film every day. My eyes would never be able to stand such a strain." It was true enough that in spite of his thick glasses, Ramesh could see only dim images on the screen. That was why, if he could help it, he avoided going to the pictures. But Usha would say, "Oh, if only I could I would see two pictures every day, especially if it is as good as Deap Kumar's *(Awara Shahzada)*. I tell you, he is a great actor...and in romantic scenes, he is really wonderful, better than even your Hollywood actors. The girls are just crazy about him."

"I can well believe it," Ramesh chuckled, "I can see one such crazy girl right here in my own home."

They were both used to such jokes at each other's expense, and neither of them minded them. So Usha retorted, "Tell me about your laboratory. I hear there are some pretty girl students who come there for research. That must be why you go there so punctually every day."

Ramesh laughed aloud. "You are quite right. But unfortunately, they don't take the slightest notice of me. So I think it would be better to carry on my research at home."

"At home? Will you set up a laboratory here?"

"Perhaps, we might have a small laboratory, too. But actually I want to do some research on a new variety of wheat seeds. For that, I should either go 10 miles out of the city to the University farm, which is difficult to manage with my present job, or I should have a little farm of my own in our bungalow compound."

"But how is that possible? We have space enough only for a few flowerbeds."

"Even that is enough...if we break up and plough through these flower beds, we can sow half a dozen samples of seeds. That's all I need for my experiments."

Usha did not like the idea at all and said so emphatically. "No, no, I will never let you break up my flowerbeds. What an idea! Destroying my beautiful roses to grow your wheat seeds! If you want to do farming, you better find some other place."

And suddenly serious, Ramesh replied, "Well, I suppose I will have to do something about that."

A week later, when he came home in the evening, Ramesh quietly informed Usha that he had been transferred to take charge of a government experimental farm near Bareilly. He did not say so, but Usha knew instinctively that Ramesh himself had asked for the transfer.

And now for a year and a half, their whole life was restricted to the boundaries of this farm. There were wheat fields on all sides so far as the eye could see. The prosaic monotonous rumble of tractors. In summer, it was too hot, in winter too cold with icy winds that came howling from the mountains. In the season of monsoons, there was water everywhere; even the roads were inundated. Their little house was literally turned into an island. Even otherwise, Usha often felt that Ramesh had brought her to a desert island just to spite her. Of course, there were several hundred farm workers, tractor-drivers, truck-drivers and others who lived in the village only half a mile away. But the fastidious, fashionable Usha refused to accept them as a substitute for the smart society of Lucknow.

Once, on the day of the festival of Holi, Ramesh took her to the village. At night, the farm workers held a big get-together—they sang local folk-songs and danced their folk-dances. Ramesh had hoped that Usha would welcome this diversion. But she, enamoured by film songs and film dances, was not likely to be impressed by the simple art of these unsophisticated village folk. The whole time she sat on her chair, aloof and disinterested, making no attempt even to hide her boredom. At the end of the programme, she and Ramesh were both garlanded—but these garlands were not made of roses or jasmine buds, but strung with ears of wheat. And a tractor-driver had nervously stuttered through a short prepared speech, "We are offering to the Director of our farm and to his wife these garlands which are made not of flowers but of ears of corn, because for us farmers, all the beauty of the world is in wheat, all the beauty and all the fragrance. In this wheat lies not only our prosperity but our whole life."

The moment she reached home, Usha threw away that prickly garland as if she was thereby discarding the whole prosaic and exasperating life of the farm.

Wheat! Wheat!! Wheat!!! Living with Ramesh, she had developed antipathy for the very word. There was talk of wheat at breakfast, at lunch, at dinner. If they went for a walk, it was through the wheat fields, and he talked of nothing else, "Look there, Usha, that is a new variety of wheat which I have grown. It has a hard, red grain, which is resistant to rust and other plant diseases," or he would say, "Look, Usha, this is American wheat, and next to that is Soviet wheat from the Ukraine, and here on an Indian farm, both are peacefully growing side by side, strictly in accordance with the five principles of co-existence. And now I am trying to grow a cross-breed which would have a grain as big as the American wheat and which would be able to withstand both heat and cold like the Soviet wheat...and it might be called 'Peace Wheat'. How do you like the idea, Usha?"

And she would burst out angrily. "Wheat! Wheat!! Wheat!!! Is there nothing else to talk about? I suppose you regard me too to be a grain of wheat."

"Of course," he would say, laughing. "There is a great deal in common between you and a grain of wheat. In wheat is the secret of human life, while you...why, you are dearer to me than life itself."

"You are a great one for empty talk," she would say, not entirely displeased with his reiteration of love, "for how long have I been asking you that the next time you go to Bareilly, bring a few cuttings or roses from someone's garden. I want to plant a rose garden here. But you either forget or don't find time for doing so."

Once more, Ramesh would promise that the next time he went to town he would positively bring a whole jeep-load of rose cuttings, and once again he would forget all about it and would have to make a fresh promise all over again. And all the time Usha's heart yearned for rose bushes as a childless woman's soul yearns to have a baby of her own in her lap.

Roses! Red, velvety roses! Little, pink rosebuds like newborn babies smiling toothlessly at the sight of their mother! It seemed that all her life's yearnings were concentrated in the colourful picture on the cover of a movie magazine. The caption read: "A view of the rose garden in Deap Kumar's home—this popular film star is a keen gardener, particularly fond of growing roses of which, there are no less than a dozen varieties in his garden. See inside for other pictures of Deap Kumar's home."

Inside, on two full pages, were special pictures of Deap Kumar's bungalow. Usha savoured each delectable detail. Pale, flower-patterned curtains in the living room. Red and blue and green cushions piled on a divan covered with black and gold embroidery. On the wall, a still-life painting of flowers by a well-known artist. An antique bronze Nataraja installed on a radiogram. A porcelain vase filled with roses on the refrigerator in the dining room. The bedroom windows opened on to the colourful panorama of the flowerbeds. "What an artistic, poetic, romantic atmosphere!" Usha mused, contrasting it with her own house. "Wherever you turn, you find ears of corn, piles of seed, odorous samples of fertilizers. In one corner there is a new type of plough designed by Ramesh; in the other lies a tractor engine opened up, all its ugly mechanical intestines strewn on the floor. Uncomfortable cane chairs instead of sofas in the living room, cots strung with hemp-rope instead of spring-beds in the bedroom. An earthen water-pitcher instead of a refrigerator, palm-leaf hand-fans instead of an air-conditioner, and instead of a radiogram, only an old-fashioned gramophone and a battery radio with its valves or battery always out of order! Really, if even today Ramesh doesn't bring the battery duly repaired...!"

In the distance, there was the sharp hooting of a jeep's electric horn which snapped the string of Usha's thoughts. She got up to receive her husband, and, quickly adjusting the folds of her sari, she ran out of the room. Ramesh must have brought the post, too, and she was anxiously waiting for her fresh weekly supply of movie magazines.

Raising a cloud of dust on what was more a dirt track than a road passing through the wheat fields, the jeep ran up to the front of the house and stopped with a screeching of brakes. On the seat beside Ramesh lay a pile of papers and letters. Usha ran down the steps of the verandah.

"Are you crazy? Running out bare-headed in the loo! Want to catch your death of sun-stroke?" Ramesh shouted at her with affectionate concern. "Get back inside or you won't get any movie magazines."

As usual, Ramesh was dressed in a khaki shirt and shorts, a sola hat pushed back on his head, sandals on his feet. His clothes and hair were covered with fine, powdery dust. The shirt, wet with perspiration, stuck to his fine, manly torso.

As he had left very early for the town, he had had no time to shave, and a tough, bristly one-day growth covered his cheeks and chin. Looking at him thus, Usha felt her old love for him and her heart sang a proud refrain, "This is my man, the beast of all men!" But the next moment, she was demanding with girlish impatience, "First tell me, have you brought all the things I wanted?"

"Yes, everything," replied Ramesh, dumping his hat on her head and then running out to unload the jeep.

"Is the battery recharged"

"Yes. Now you can listen in to all that musical nonsense from Radio Ceylon."

"And cold cream?

"Here is your cream, too, but I am afraid on the way it has melted into hot oil."

"What else have you brought for me?"

"Nothing else except your magazines and some things for the farm, some new samples of vegetable seeds and cuttings of some plants."

"But you would never remember to bring for me cuttings of some rose bushes!" she pouted with her old complaint.

"Don't worry about your rose bushes. One day, by magic you will find a whole rose garden in full bloom right here under your window. But now come in. I want to tell you something important."

Ramesh took off his shirt, hung it out to dry, and went into the bathroom to splash a whole bucket of cold water on his face and head and arms. Then, rubbing himself vigorously with a towel, he came out and selected a long, official-looking envelope from the pile of letters.

"Read this," he said giving it to Usha, "I am afraid we are in for a lot of bother. A film company is arriving here next week to shoot some scenes on the farm, and the government wants us to give them all our facilities as it is official policy to encourage production of such films about national projects and so on. It seems like a boring business to me, not to mention the dislocation of our work on the farm, but I bet you will be quite pleased."

"Not likely," Usha said disinterestedly, taking out the letter from the envelope. "They will be the same old newsreel people: dull old cameramen who will depart after photographing the tractors and the ploughs from every angle."

"But first read the name of company that is coming," said Ramesh teasingly. "Then tell me if your heart doesn't beat faster."

Usha read the letter, "'A unit of Deap Kumar Productions, Ltd., will be arriving to shoot their film, *Naya Hindustan.* ' This means that..."

"It means that your favorite actor-director-producer, the great, the one and only Deap Kumar, conqueror of a million feminine hearts, is coming here in person."

And Usha was as excited as a schoolgirl, "Really, Ramesh? It will be great fun." And then the woman in her introduced the eternal feminine problem. "But I have not even one decent sari. When these people come, what shall I wear?"

DEAP KUMAR

"Mr. Deap Kumar, what is the name of our new film?"

"*Naya Hindustan.*"

"And is it true that much of it is going to be shot outdoors, on an agricultural farm?"

"Yes, that is correct."

"Can you tell us something about the film?"

"Certainly. You see, in this film we want to show the important changes in the lives of our people which have taken place since our country became free in 1947. The location of this film is a model farm where the hero, an educated farmer, teaches peasants new methods of agriculture and helps to create a new life in the village..."

This interview was taking place on a platform of the Bombay Central Station in front of an air-conditioned coupe. The other members of the Deap Kumar Productions unit, including the heroine, Alkarani, her Anglo-Indian hair-dresser Julie, cameraman Bhaskar and sound engineer Desai had all taken their seats in their respective compartments. Only Deap Kumar stood on the platform, surrounded by journalists and a crowd of admirers. But when his secretary Waman Rao reminded him that there were only five minutes more for the train to start, Deap

Kumar joined his hands in an elaborate and self-conscious gesture of salutation and asked to be excused. "If you don't mind, gentlemen, I must take your leave now. I have to say farewell to some other friends, too," saying this amidst the cheers of the more enthusiastic film fans present, Deap Kumar, the idol of millions, entered his reserved coupe, and the door was closed.

"Well, Paro, won't you change your mind even now? We have this whole coupe to ourselves, both seats are reserved for us. Why don't you come along? They can send your clothes by plane tomorrow."

"No, darling, you go with your unit and do your work and I will look after the children. If I go with you, it will unnecessarily affect your reputation and your popularity."

"What do you mean? Is it a sin or a crime for a wife to travel with her husband?"

"Not in the case of ordinary people. But remember, you are a film star. At every station, the crowds will gather to have a glimpse of their favourite actor, most of them adolescent girls from schools and colleges. If they discover that their dream hero is so commonplace as to be not only prosaically married but even taking his wife with him, it will be a terrible blow to all their romantic illusions. It will damage your reputation as the heartthrob of millions. It might be even fatal to your whole career."

Deap Kumar knew that what Parvati was saying was basically true. But in the way she expressed it, he could feel the slight pinch of sarcasm. After five years of marriage, he still loved her, and he know that she also loved him. But he suspected—and gradually the suspicion was turning into conviction—that she was not greatly impressed by the great actor-director-producer Deap.

Perhaps she did not even respect him. Often, he had the feeling that she was laughing at him, making fun of his "great artist" pose. Sometimes she treated him as elders treat children or the wise ones treat the dull-witted. And then he became conscious of a deep void in his life—as if, in spite of his fabulous wealth, he was a pauper; as if, in spite of his enormous popularity, he was an unknown upstart; as if, in spite of the fact that film journals called him a genius, he was but a fool and an ignoramus.

The fact was that in his relations with his wife, Deap suffered from an inferiority complex. She was more beautiful than any of his heroines. Her father was a rich and famous solicitor of Bombay, while his own father, until two years ago, had a watch-repairing shop in Chandni Chowk of Delhi. She had done her MA in English Literature, while he was only an undergraduate. With her father, she had toured the whole of Europe, and talked of the Louvre in Paris, the St. Paul's in Rome or the Hyde Park of London as casually as if some Bombayite might be mentioning Dadar or Mahim or Kalbadevi, while Deap had not seen any city even in India beyond Delhi and Bombay. The entire film press published reviews and articles (many of them, of course, written by his own publicity manager), praising the acting of Deap Kumar as a subtle combination of Raj Kapoor and Dilip Kumar, comparing him to Clark Gable and James Stewart. But when he came home, his wife talked learnedly about the historic achievements of Laurence Olivier's Hamlet or Cherkasov's Alexander Nevsky in such a way that, by comparison, Deap could not but feel hopelessly inferior. When the critics praised his *Tenement Number Twelve* as a masterpiece of realism, Parvati only said, "Why do you want to court bankruptcy by imitating the Italians?" And when his *Awara Shahzada* broke all box-office records, all that his wife said was, "Well, at least it will pay off your debts."

But now, by producing *Naya Hindustan*, Deap wanted to impress his wife, more than anyone else, with his artistic vision and his social conscience. He was going to make it altogether different from any film ever produced in India. Most of the shooting would be outdoors on actual locations. Real peasants, and not professional extras, would work in the crowd scenes. He had persuaded the government to give him facilities to shoot some of the scenes on a model agricultural farm. He wanted Parvati to go with him on this expedition so that once and for all, she could be convinced that her husband was not just a cheap actor and commercial producer but an inspired and sincere artist with a deep understanding of the potentialities of his art. But Parvati did not agree. She said, "If I go, who will look after the children? And it is too hot to take them on such a long journey."

"All right, then," said Deap when the guard blew his whistle, "Goodbye, darling. Kiss Junior and Jammo for me, and send me a telegram every day, or I will be worried about the children."

"And you also look after yourself," said Parvati as she got up. "Keep a hat on your head when shooting in the sun, and drink a lot of lemon squash to guard against sun-stroke." Then, with a maternal gesture, she ruffled Deap's artificially-waved hair, patted his cheek and got down from the compartment just as the train began to move. And for a moment, Deap had a feeling of helplessness, almost of panic, like a child leaving his mother for the first time and starting on a long journey, and he thought, "How will I manage without Paro for so many days?"

The train was now thundering through the city and through the double-glass windows of the coupe, the lights on the station and on the roads along the railway track looked like torches held aloft by a flying demon army.

Mahalaxmi, Lower Parel, Elphinstone Bridge...one station passed after another in quick succession. The train was going towards Delhi at 50 miles per hour, and at the same breathless speed, Deap's imagination was racing backwards across the years.

Dadar–Matunga Road–Mahim–Bandra–

1955–1954–1953–1952–Khar–Santa Cruz–Vile Parle–Andheri–1951–1950–1949–1948–It was eight years ago that he had come to Bombay from Delhi.

But then he was not Deap Kumar the famous actor. He was Suraj Narain Mathur, an unemployed undergraduate. And he had travelled not by an air-conditioned coupe but by Third Class. That was only eight years ago but it seemed like 8,000 years.

The train had passed through the suburbs, rumbled over the bridges, over the creeks, and was now rolling across the flat, limitless plain. The moonlit landscape, with its dark silhouettes of trees and huts, was racing backwards like his memory and, after a while, it seemed to him that the film of his past was unrolling itself on the glass screen of his coupe window.

1948—when he was rudely turned out of the Hindustan Film Studio because he had trespassed without permission and because his clothes were dirty and torn and he had not eaten for two days, he had dark rings around his eyes and, with his overgrown beard, he looked more like a tramp than the famous actor of the future.

1949—when, at last, he did get a job: as an assistant in the Popular Shoe Mart. The whole day, it was his business to sit at other people's feet and find the proper size shoes for them. Dirty feet, flat feet, dainty feet, odorous and sweaty feet! He even dreamt of feet in those days. In one of his dreams, he saw himself being trampled to death by millions of gigantic feet. But one day, the telephone bell rang in the shop and set in motion a series of events which were soon going to release him forever from a life of poverty and putrid feet.

"Suraj!" the fat proprietor of the Shoe Mart called to the assistant who would one day be known as Deap Kumar. "Find all the fancy ladies' sandals in number four size and take them to the Ideal Film Studio to Miss Radha Rani. She wants to buy some shoes for her new film."

And then for the second time, he got into a film studio and, this time, he was not turned out because he had come in a taxi and was representing the Popular Shoe Mart. The moment he presented his firm's card at the enquiry-window, he was led to the great Miss Radha Rani's dressing room.

"I tell you I won't act with him. I won't! I won't!! I won't!!! Can't you see that he has become quite bald now? He will look like my father!"

Radha Rani was shouting at Director Desai when Deap (who was still called Suraj) timidly opened the door.

"Madam, I have come from the Popular Shoe Mart." For a moment, Radha Rani did not reply but kept looking at him…as if he was a queer fish. Then she said, "Good. Let's see if you have some decent sandals."

As Deap opened the boxes and tried different sandals on Radha Rani's feet, she kept arguing with the director about the choice of a hero for her new film. One was bald, the other was fat, one was too tall, the other too short. The ones she liked were too busy with other pictures or demanded fabulous amounts which the producer was not able to afford.

"If that is the case," she said in exasperation, "why don't you try a newcomer?"

"But where am I to get a suitable newcomer? You talk as if it was not a hero but a shoe we needed."

"After all, what is the difference? Both heroes and shoes must be discarded when they become old and worn out. In their place, we must get new shoes and new heroes... Yes, this one will do. It fits me." This she said to Deap, who was trying a pair on her feet, but evidently she meant to convey something to the director, too, for five minutes later, Deap went to Desai, who asked him point-blank, "Well, Mister, would you like to work in our film?" And Suraj, who had dreamed of this moment for many years, could only answer, "Yes-yes-yes-please get me a glass of water. I feel dizzy."

1950—when Suraj Narain Mathur had been transformed into Deap Kumar, and he was working simultaneously in seven pictures, and he had more than a hundred thousand rupees of "black money" in the locker of his bank! One evening, he drove his swanky Buick convertible to the Malabar Hill mansion of his solicitor, Kikachand Premchand. Deap himself now lived in an expensive flat overlooking the sea in Worli, but he had never seen such a magnificent and beautifully-furnished house. Not only wealth (which Deap did not lack now) but a cultivated good taste was apparent from everything in the place—bookshelves that covered whole walls, fine original paintings by world-famous artists, thick Persian carpets, modernistic furniture, antique bronzes, Kathiawari tapestries and a wall-length window through which could be seen the entire panorama of the city and the lovely blue bay. And when, after the business talk, the solicitor introduced his daughter, Parvati, it seemed to Deap that all the beauty and good taste of that house was summed up and symbolised in the slim, beautiful and intelligent girl who could, with equal ease and casualness, prepare *pakoda*s in the kitchen, pour out tea for the guest in the drawing room, and talk learnedly about the poetry of Byron and the short stories of Chekhov. Deap, who had never seen such a house nor met such a girl, felt that all his wealth and popularity were of no value whatsoever if he could not have a wife like Parvati to share his life.

1951—when he married Parvati and started his own company, Deap Kumar Productions.

1952—when their first child was born, who was named Jagdeep (but who was called "Junior" by the mother) and when Deap Kumar Productions' very first film *Aasmani Chudiyaan* celebrated its silver jubilee, giving Deap a net profit of nearly half a million rupees, and Deap began the construction of his own studio. It was in the same year that they had their first quarrel when Parvati refused to attend the premiere of his second production, *Hai Mere Balam*, saying, "For a successful actor-director-producer like you, it is better to keep your home life separate from your professional activities," and later, when Deap showed her the film at home and asked if she liked it, she only said, "What does my opinion matter? The public likes it, doesn't it? That's what matters."

1953—when their second child was born and named Jamma (but the parents lovingly called her "Jammo"), and *Hai Mere Balam* celebrated its golden jubilee and Deap bought a bungalow and spent a quarter million rupees on renovating and furnishing it, and growing the finest rose garden in Bombay.

1954—when Deap Kumar Productions' *Tenement Number Twelve* won critical acclaim as a realistic masterpiece, but failed at the box-office, thus helping adjust the huge profits of *Awara Shahzada*, and Deap's roses got the first prize in the flower-show, and Junior went to kindergarten for the first time, and Jammo began to lisp "Papa-Mummy", and Deap got a liquor permit for two units of whiskey on the strength of a doctor's certificate which declared that he needed alcoholic sustenance because of creative and financial worries...

1955—the train stopped with a jerk and the reel of his reminiscences was violently snapped. A waiter from the dining car knocked and enquired if he needed any dinner, but Deap ordered only two bottles of soda.

As the train started again, he took out the bottle of whiskey from the suitcase and poured himself a double peg. Then he took out a folding leather picture-frame which was always with him.

He looked at Junior and Jammo and, between them, Parvati smiling.

"Well, Paro, here's to you!" he raised his glass and gulped it down.

After the fifth peg, he looked at Parvati's photograph and murmured, "Why do you laugh at me, Paro? Why do you make fun of me? Is it because my father was a poor watch-repairer and yours an eminent solicitor? Or because I am not even a graduate while you are an MA in English Literature? Or because you are a cultured person who likes classical music, Bharatanatyam, Russian Ballet and Italian films, while I produce cheap and vulgar films like *Awara Shahzada* and *Aasmani Chudiyaan* to make money?"

After the seventh peg, he glared at her picture with red-rimmed eyes. "The whole world respects me as a great artiste, millions praise my work, wherever I go there are crowds round me, I get thousands of appreciative fan letters every month, but you don't respect me, Paro! You don't regard me even as your equal—you think I am crude and cheap, an illiterate buffoon?"

After the ninth peg, he addressed her picture again, "What do you think you are, Parvati? Admittedly, you are beautiful and intelligent, highly educated, much-travelled, the daughter of an aristocratic family. But does it give you the right to laugh at me, to hold your husband in such utter contempt? Don't laugh at me, Paro, don't laugh at me...please...please! I can't bear it..."

But his drunken voice went no further than the soundproof coupe, and when he had drugged himself to sleep, Parvati's photograph continued to smile, in a way in which there was sarcasm and ridicule but also love and pity!

RAMESH

Holding the steering wheel of the tractor with both his strong hands, Ramesh could feel the throbbing of the powerful engine. Whenever he drove a tractor, he felt a strange and overwhelming sensation, a feeling of triumphant joy, as if he was not the director of a farm, but the commander of a victorious army, pursuing a defeated enemy, and that he was driving not a tractor but a tank, the sharp mechanical sickles of his harvester combine against the tallest crop in the biggest wheat field.

The combine attached to the tractor was going through the crop as a barber's machine goes through a man's thick hair. He smiled at his simile and thought that it was not poetic enough. Krishen Chander, in one of his stories, has compared the farmer's sickle with the pen of the writer and the brush of the artist, for, with his sickle, the farmer created both beauty and art on the canvas of the earth. And, he thought, if the sickle was the pen of the old peasant, then the combine was the typewriter of the farmer of today on which the story of the new man was being tapped out. No, even this simile did not satisfy him. He wished he was a writer or an artist to express this strange and beautiful and intoxicating feeling about the historic, world-shaking significance of mechanised agriculture. Ten years ago, it took hundreds of peasants and their women and children at least 10 days to harvest the crop in such a big field. But now, it could be done by a tractor and a combine in a few hours. And he felt that much more important than the Revolution which the politicians created with their fiery speeches was the revolution that these machines were bringing about in the life of millions of peasants—machines that, in other countries, had released man forever from hard, animal-like labour, that were increasing the world production of food grains, and that eventually would change the very face of their own country. More than anyone else, perhaps, Ramesh could feel this change coming over the

Indian countryside which had stood rooted in the past for many thousand years...

Ahead of him, to the left, he could see their farm's second tractor being driven by Gangoo—the 18-year-old peasant boy whose forefathers, for hundreds of years, had lived the life of serfs, ploughing the landlord's fields, sowing the landlord's fields, and harvesting the landlord's fields, working with primitive ploughs and sickles made by the village blacksmith who had never even travelled by train to the town of Bareilly only 60 miles away. But today, Gangoo is the best tractor-driver of the farm; he can read and write, wears shirt and shorts and a hat like Ramesh. His old father, constitutionally and legally free from serfdom, still talks to government officials and to the sons of the landlord in servile, cringing tones, a habit which is a hangover from the feudal past. But Gangoo speaks a different language, in different tones. He has travelled 500 miles up to Bhopal where in six months, the peasant-boy was transformed into a skilled mechanic at the Central Tractor Organisation. Since then, every morning he reads a Hindi newspaper, every evening he listens to the radio, every week he goes to Bareilly to see a film.

You don't find him cringing before anyone. If only he was an artist, thought Ramesh, he would have made a painting of Gangoo and called it "The New Indian Peasant". He would have shown him driving his tractor, his dark, tough body wet with the perspiration of harvest toil, his strong peasant's hands gripping the wheel, face lit up, his eyes on the distant horizon. The background of this portrait of Gangoo was picturesque, too. The golden sun-kissed wheat crop gently swayed in the breeze, like waves in the sea. To the north, behind the dark silhouettes of the mango groves, were the dim outlines of the hills which were slowly melting into soft-brown clouds. There is no more beautiful view in the whole wide world, thought Ramesh, nor is there any music sweeter than the whirring of the tractor, for in this music, there is power, an iron rhythm, and the message of a new life.

"Cut?"

A vague and muffled cry echoed from another world, but failed to interrupt the stream of Ramesh's thoughts. A whistle blew, but somehow Ramesh could not imagine that it had anything to do with him. He continued to drive his tractor, the combine went on revolving, and its mechanical sickles went on cutting the crop. Ahead of him, the sky was aflame with red and orange clouds, and the last rays of the setting sun were kissing the flowing wheat-crop with a touch of gold.

"Cut! Cut!" The echoes from the other world sounded nearer, more urgent. Whistles blew shrilly, wildly. But Ramesh's hand did not move towards the brake. His conqueror's chariot continued triumphantly to cut its way through the hosts of the enemy…

"Stop the tractor!"

Someone shouted very near to him, and it was only then that Ramesh turned and looked. It was an assistant of Deap Kumar, and behind him, running, panting, slipping on the carpet of harvested crop, came the great actor-director-producer. Ramesh pulled the hand brake, and as he switched off the engine. With a jerk, his mind returned to the reality of the moment.

"My dear chap," shouted Deap, "what are you doing? Why didn't you listen? The whole shot is spoilt. Can't you see there is no light in this part of the field? So now we must cut to a mid-shot."

Only now did Ramesh remember that he was not just harvesting the crop but taking part in a shot for Deap Kumar's film *Naya Hindustan*. As the actor could not handle the tractor with the touch of an expert, he had requested Ramesh to drive it in the long shot. They were both of about the same height, and Deap, too, appeared in the scene in a khaki shirt, shorts and a hat so no one could make out the difference. In the next and closer shot, Deap would be shown applying the brake and getting off the tractor.

"Thank you, anyway," said Deap, jumping into the driving seat on the tractor. "If you don't mind, just start the engine, and explain how one must apply the brakes. I think I can manage the rest."

Ramesh explained the function of the different levers and climbed down from the machine. The cameraman was setting up his camera in a new position. Behind him was the crowd of the actors and assistants and among them stood Usha, fascinated by every detail of the shooting.

"Did you see, Usha?" Ramesh asked, wiping away the sweat from his neck, "I have become a film star now."

"*Hain!* What did you say?" she asked absentmindedly. Her eyes were focused on Deap.

"Nothing, I only wanted to tell you that I am going back home. I want to listen to the weather report on the radio. If you like, you can stay on and watch the shooting." And he strode on through the fields.

The next shot was now being taken. Gangoo started the engine, then jumped off, and Deap took charge of the tractor and drove it for a few yards; then, just as the famous voice of Lata Mangeshkar was heard through the playback machine, singing the theme song of the film, Deap turned back, reacted with a smile, applied the brakes, and, jumping off the tractor, ran over the harvested crop towards the part of the field which was not yet cut. The camera panned to follow him and from the wheat field appeared the heroine, Alkarani, in a silk-and-crepe version of the village maiden's dress, calling out in Lata Mangeshkar's voice, "O-o-o-o." Deap pursued her, she hid behind the crop, he followed her there, she emerged from hiding, tantalising him with another "O-o-o-o," Deap caught up with her, holding her by the wrist. The playback machine cried in the voice of Lata Mangeshkar, "Chhodo…Chhodoji Meri Kaliyya" (Let go of my dainty wrist, let go) but Alkarani forgot to synchronise her lip-movement with the played-back voice, and the assistant director shouted. "Cut! Cut!!" Deap looked at his watch. The cameraman raised his eyes towards the darkening sky, and Deap announced, "Shooting pack-up." Alkarani pulled at her plaits of artificial hair and, throwing them to Julie, shouted, "Come on, darling, let's go and have a cold-water bath." The second assistant director ran up to with her sandals, and Alkarani was on her way to the camp, her anklet-bells ringing as she walked.

"Are you coming, Mrs. Ramesh Chandra?" Deap addressed his hostess with formal courtesy.

"Yes, let's go." There was the merest hint of excitement in her voice.

The narrow high path cut through the wheat fields. The big red ball of the sun was sinking below the horizon. Deap was silent out of polite discretion and Usha out of nervousness at being alone with the screen idol of the millions.

Then, she said, "Mr. Deap Kumar, how can you do so many things? I mean, you not only act, but also direct and produce films. It is really remarkable."

Deap smiled the famous smile which, when flashed on the screen, disturbed so many feminine hearts. "There is nothing remarkable about doing several jobs if none of them is done well."

"Do you want me to flatter you? Believe me, I like your pictures so much—so much—I have not missed a single one of them. You are really wonderful."

And suddenly, Deap wished he had heard those words uttered by Parvati. But to Usha, he said, "Then please tell me in which capacity you like my work better—as an actor or as a director?"

She thought for a moment as they walked in silence, then she spoke, "I will tell you. As a director, you seem to have absorbed all the pain and sorrow of the world in your own heart. Whatever aspect of life you depict, you do it with the fullest sympathy. In *Tenement Number Twelve*, you have realistically portrayed life in the slums. In *Awara Shahzada* when the prince, disguised as a bandit, robs the rich and distributes their wealth among the poor, it is really a very effective scene. And then the songs. They are always a speciality of your films."

"And as an actor?"

"As an actor, you are even greater. Whatever role you play, you merge your own personality in it. But you come out best in romantic scenes. If you don't mind, may I say something?"

"By all means. I am very interested in all you are saying."

"The girls in our college used to say that when a girl sees you making love on the screen, it seems to her so real as if it was to her that you were..." She felt too shy to complete the sentence.

"...making love! Is that it?"

She nodded.

For some minutes, they walked without speaking, their footfalls lost in the all-pervading silence of the wheat fields. The sun had set but an afterglow lingered in the sky. A shepherd's flute sounded softly sweet in the distance. The magic of that twilight hour, the presence of this beautiful and slim young woman by his side, the silky rustle of her sari, the sweetly pungent aroma of the attar of roses, the shy and sweet compliments she had paid him—Deap was overwhelmed by a feeling of happiness, of tenderness and strange satisfaction, which he had never felt before. It seemed to him that he was at last overcoming the supreme frustration of his life.

He stopped to light a cigarette. It was quite dark now and he could see only the silhouette of her profile. But as the lighter threw up its little flame, he saw her very close: the classic oval of her face, the smooth, olive-complexioned skin, and those dark and limpid eyes looking up to him with such undisguised admiration. Finding him looking at her, she modestly lowered her eyelids. Deap's hand crept towards Usha's waist, then thinking better of it, he withdrew it to his side. They resumed their walk, the winding path ahead of them only dimly visible in the starlight.

"Tell me, please, about your life here on the farm."

"Our life is hardly worth talking about, Deap *ji*."

"You can cut out this '*ji*' business. All my friends call me Deap."

"You are an expert in psychology. You can understand what kind of life one can lead in such an atmosphere, cut off from the world. Colourless, tasteless, purposeless—that's my life."

"Why don't you take up some work, then? You are educated, after all."

"But not sufficiently educated, you see. I was still an undergraduate when I got married, and even to be a teacher, one must be a graduate... But why are you laughing? Do I sound ridiculous?"

"No, no, I was laughing because I, too, am only an undergraduate. Yet, I do manage to work."

"But your case is different. You work in films."

"Well, you too can work in films."

"Who? Me?" And to Usha it seemed as if suddenly the world was resounding with joyous bells, as if all that exasperating expanse of wheat fields had suddenly been transformed into a rose garden!

"But who would give me work in films, Deap *ji*?"

"Just call me Deap, and perhaps even I might give you work in my films, Usha."

"Really, Deap? You are not joking?"

"No, I am quite serious. You see, to be successful as a film star you need two things—beauty and intelligence. Most of our actresses are only beautiful—some are now not even that. Look at poor Alkarani. She is carrying on on the strength of her reputation of 10 years ago. But you are lucky in being both intelligent and beautiful."

"Are you sure you are not joking? Please be serious. It is a matter which might affect my whole life."

"No, Usha, I am not joking. But perhaps I should not have said what I have. This is how film directors are supposed to entice innocent girls. I wonder what your husband will say when he hears of it."

"I am his wife, not his slave-girl. I can do what I like."

Now they had reached the bungalow. There was light inside and they could hear the sputtering atmospherics of the radio punctuating the news bulletin. Just near the bungalow was Deap's camp—four tents: one for Deap, one for Alkarani and Julia, one for the technicians and the fourth for the junior staff.

Usha bade him farewell in a self-consciously loud voice. "All right, Mr. Deap Kumar, you go and have a wash. I will be sending you tea straight away."

"Thank you, Mrs. Ramesh Chandra, I am afraid we cause you so much trouble."

Usha went into the room where Ramesh sat near the radio, intently listening to the news. From a far distance came a rumble of thunder and a streak of lightning flashed across the sky. But still Usha did not imagine that a storm was imminent.

The radio announcer was saying, "According to a statement issued by the Food Ministry, this year, our production of food grains is expected to be higher than any previous year. If the record wheat crop, which is now ripe, is harvested before the rains come, then it might be safely assumed that we have achieved self-sufficiency in food and that there is no fear of famine or shortage in any part of the country..."

"Did you hear that, Usha?" Ramesh greeted his wife with a smile. "Our farm is ahead of all others in harvesting. If only these film people had not been interfering with our work for the past week, by today we would have harvested the entire crop. I am quite sure our farm this year is going to set up a record of wheat production per acre."

"Can you ever talk of anything except the wheat crop and harvesting? At least sometimes you must think of me, too."

"Why, what has happened? You are not feeling well? I hope it's not a sunstroke. You have been out in the sun the whole day. You haven't had a moment's rest for a whole week. God knows when we shall be free of the boredom of these film people."

He was taken aback by her violent reply. Suddenly, she cried out. "They are not bores—they are very interesting people, making a good film. You are a bore—with your perpetual talk of seeds and fertilisers and crops and ploughs and tractors! There is nothing else in the world that you can talk about."

"Usha!" he exclaimed with more surprise that anger. "What has happened to you today?" Just then, there was a blinding flash of lightning outside in the dark sky, and a moment later the house itself shook with a clap of thunder.

"Ramesh, I am going to Bombay."

At first, he did not understand what she was talking about. "What do you say? Bombay? But why? When?"

Usha turned her face to the window, looking into the darkness. "I am going to work in films. Deap—Mr. Deap Kumar—has offered to star me in his films."

"Oh, so that's it." Ramesh laughed, somewhat relieved. "So the great Deap Kumar wants to make you into a film star. Well, congratulations. Now you too can dress yourself in a silken version of the village maiden's dress like Alkarani, and sing songs to lure tractor-driving heroes. But don't forget to invite me to the premiere. By the way, what will be your first film—*Thief of Baghdad* or *Wild Cat of Bombay*?"

"Ramesh!" Her voice was like a roll of thunder. "I am not joking. It is true. I am fed up of this place, this life, of everything."

"Fed up with this life? But why?"

"Because wheat is not everything in life, one needs roses, too!"

"So you want to plant some rose bushes. But I have already..."

Interrupting him, she cried out, "I am not talking of a few rose bushes. I am referring to my whole life. You have brought me to this farm and imprisoned me here, where there is no decent place to live, no decent clothes to wear, no decent people to meet—only ignorant, uncultured village yokels. I can't go to the pictures or to the club or for shopping. Here, there is only the maddening gharr-gharr-gharr of your tractors, the eternal stink of your beloved fertilisers. You have made my life useless, purposeless."

Ramesh did not often lose his temper, but when he did, he could explode with anger. "You fool! You call this life purposeless? You regard wheat-growing a nuisance? You dare to look down upon those simple peasants? But do you know it is to them and millions like them that you owe your life? If they were to stop working tomorrow, what would you eat? How could you live? Instead of bread, will you eat your precious roses?"

Once again there was a flash of lightning, and for a moment, the room was flooded with a blinding glare of unnatural light like a flood-lit stage or film studio during shooting—and in that moment, Ramesh and Usha did not look like a real husband and wife, but appeared as the grease-painted hero and heroine, striking theatrical poses in a scene of passion from an old-fashioned play. But then the flash was gone, leaving the room in darkness, and there was such an explosion of thunder that Usha was frightened into an involuntary and characteristically feminine "Ooi!"

"Special bulletin for farmers"—the radio was calling out. "Special bulletin for farmers. In the foothills and lowlands of Uttar Pradesh, a thunderstorm accompanied by strong winds and rain is expected tonight. All farmers are warned to complete as much harvesting as they can tonight and properly store the harvested crop or they are likely to lose it in the storm. Twelve inches of rainfall has been recorded during the last 24 hours in the Kumaon hills and so there is also the danger of floods in the rivers of this region. All villagers in the low-lying regions near the rivers are warned to keep an all-night vigil."

"Oh, my god!" Ramesh cried out, "Our harvest may be ruined!" At that moment, he forgot the violent quarrel he was just having with his wife. He remembered only one thing—the harvest, the harvest!

In the verandah hung a brass gong to be sounded in such an emergency. The farm workers were instructed to collect at the director's bungalow the moment they heard the alarm. Ramesh took the iron rod and furiously beat the gong, and the metallic vibrations went forth across the farm. Within a few minutes, his men began to arrive, all running with a sense of urgency, and Gangoo was the first.

"Gangoo, collect everyone on the farm!" Ramesh issued orders like a commander on a battlefield. "The harvested wheat that lies in the fields must be carried to the barns before it starts to rain, and the crop that is left standing has to be harvested right now. You take one tractor and combine and I will take the other. Tell all the women and children to take out their sickles and start using them. Somehow, we have got to complete the harvesting before the rain spoils our crop."

"Yes, Ramesh Babu, but....."

"Gangoo, I don't want to hear any 'buts'. It has to be done."

"But, *huzoor*, how shall we do any harvesting in the dark?" This was Gangoo's old father speaking humbly, with folded hands.

And Ramesh received a blow of acute disappointment as if, on the eve of battle, a General was informed that his army had no ammunition. How were they to face the enemy?

A thoughtful, anxious silence fell on the whole crowd. Then someone spoke out from the rear, "Will it do if we flood-lit the field?"

Everyone turned around to look. It was Deap Kumar in an exotic silk dressing gown and he was saying, "After all, what else are our generators and arc lamps for?"

"Arc lamps!" Ramesh exclaimed, incredulously, hopefully.

"How many have you got?"

"Eight—they should be sufficient for the portion of the field that is to be cut." Then he shouted to his assistants, "Come on, hurry up, tell our electricians to set up the arcs all round the field," Then he took off his dressing gown, flung it aside and, catching hold of Ramesh by the hand, ran out towards the fields. Soon everyone was gone and only Usha was left behind. She knew now that for the moment, she was forgotten both by Ramesh and Deap.

The field was a field of battle. The arc lamps had floodlit quite a big area and, in their light, the combines attached to Ramesh's and Gangoo's tractors were harvesting the wheat. As an auxiliary irregular force, more than a hundred men, women and children were cutting down the crop with their sickles. The rest of the people, carrying bundles of wheat sheaves, were running towards the barns. Dark, menacing clouds were massing in the sky, there were frequent flashes of lightning, and the air was getting colder and damper, bringing the threat of imminent rain. Any moment, the downpour could start, or a strong wind could blow away the wheat that still lay on the ground. Every man, woman and child had only one thought—the crop must be saved! Ramesh was grimly tense and taut, as if it was not a tractor but a tank that he was driving. But Gangoo was cheerful and gay, even humming a folk song. In the light of the arcs he saw, directly ahead of his tractor, that Gori, the village headman's daughter, was plying her sickle with practised, rhythmic strides. How beautiful she looked in that light—Gori, who had been Gangoo's childhood playmate but who had recently acquired a shy and coy and altogether tantalising reserve, even pulling down the veil of her scarf whenever Gangoo was present! "*Eh,* Gori, get out of the way! Here comes Gangoo Maharaj on his royal chariot!" he shouted, laughing and exultant. But today Gori, too, was transformed. She stood up, cheerfully defiant with the sickle in her hand, beads of perspiration on her plump, bare arms and her forehead glistening in the yellow light. "Go your way, Mister," she mocked him. "Gori's sickle is harvesting more wheat than your wonderful machine."

A little farther away, Gangoo's old father was wielding his ancient sickle with his wrinkled, dried-up hands. Near him were Gori's little brother and sister, Gopal and Rajji, pecking away with their own child-sized sickles.

And watching all this was Usha who stood alone and aloof, unnoticed by anyone because she was right under a giant-sized arc lamp. For the first time in her life, she was struck by the uneasy thought that everyone else was working and only she was idle, useless, a virtual cripple!

She saw an old woman, her myopic, aged eyes blinded by the direct glare of the arcs, wielding the sickle with a trembling hand while with the other she groped for the wheat stalks to cut. Usha was afraid the old woman might slash at her own hand.

"Mother, give this to me, and you rest for a while," she said, gently taking away the sickle. But soon she learnt that it was not such an easy work as it had seemed to her. Sitting on the ground, her legs became cramped, her silk sari was torn as it got caught in some thorns, her hands and arms got scratches. More that once, she slashed with the sickle, but the angle was wrong and so the blade slipped on the stalk-roots, and once, instead of the wheat, she cut her own hand. "*Hai,* Ram!" she thought, "Am I really so useless that I can't do this simple work which even children are doing so easily?" Gori's little sister, Rajji, caught her by the hand and said, "No, Auntie, not like that, but like this," demonstrating the correct angle at which the sickle had to be handled.

"Get out of the way!" shouted Ramesh when he saw the silhouette of a woman seated right in the path of his tractor. And then, as he recognised her, he exclaimed with sudden joy. "Usha, is that really you?"

"Why not?" she replied, with a new kind of pride. "Do you think I cannot do even this much work?"

"Well done, but now only a little bit remains to be harvested and our combines can manage it in no time. You get all the women to carry the wheat they have cut to the barns. Hurry up—it has already begun to drizzle."

Usha felt a couple of raindrops fall on her hands, and she shouted, "Come on, come on, hurry up. The rain is coming." She saw that Gori was trying to lift a huge load of wheat and ran to help her.

As the raindrops began to fall, everyone felt the urgency of the moment and worked faster. The sickles began to fly, the tractors roared with speed and those who were carrying bundles of the crop began to run to the barns and back.

And then came the moment of final triumph as Ramesh and Gangoo's tractors laid low the last bit of the standing crop. Now it had begun to drizzle; the wind too was gaining in velocity, but the crop had been saved in time. Not a grain of wheat was lost.

"Gangoo!" shouted Ramesh, "Turn back now or the tractors will be ruined by the rain."

The downpour came with a sudden cloudburst, and with the sharp blast of a whistle, Deap's voice rang out, "Cut!" Ramesh looked back and saw Deap getting drenched while he held an umbrella over the camera.

"Did you film all this?" Ramesh asked, and did not try to hide the annoyance in his tone.

"Yes, of course, one doesn't get such exciting action every day. It has given us a terrific new climax."

And Ramesh, exhausted after the strain, thought, "Damn these film folk. They look at everything only from their cinematic angle—be it famine, fire or flood—they keep on cranking their cameras and searching for their stupid climaxes!" But aloud he said, "I thought in your climax the hero was to jump off the tractor and run after the heroine."

"All that is changed—now this will be the climax."

It was pouring from the heavens in a torrent. Usha, whose torn sari now clung to her rain-soaked body, shouted from a distance, "For God's sake, have your discussion at home. Do you both want to catch pneumonia?"

"Ramesh Babu! Ramesh Babu!" someone came running from the riverside.

"What is it, Matadin?"

Before the panting Matadin could reply, an arc light exploded with a bang, as a raindrop fell on the overheated glass, and the next moment all the lights were fused.

Matadin's voice was heard in the dark, "Ramesh Babu, the water in the river has come up to the flood-level. The embankment just above our farm night crack any moment."

For just such an emergency, Ramesh had kept hundreds of sandbags ready on the farm. He shouted to Matadin. "Get some people and bring the sandbags to the embankment. I am going to the spot."

There was a flash of lighting and he saw that Usha and Deap were still standing there, getting soaked in the rain. "Usha, you go home. And Mr. Deap Kumar too. Get your people and things out of the tents and in our house."

"My boys will see to that," replied Deap. "Mr. Ramesh can inform them. But I am coming with you."

It was dark again and Ramesh could not see Deap but he spoke to the dark form beside him. "This is dangerous work, Mr. Deap Kumar. It is not a scene for film heroes."

When he reached the embankment, he saw that his farm workers were already rushing there with sandbags on their backs. Ramesh took no time in locating the crack in the embankment from where a stream of flooded water was already rushing down to menace the lowland of the farm. Ramesh got the breach filled and reinforced with sandbags, and when lightning briefly illuminated the scene of action, he was surprised to see Deap among the people who were placing the sandbags. Angrily, he shouted above the roar of the waters, "Mr. Deap, what on earth are you doing here? Go home and sleep. If something happens to you, I will be blamed."

But before Deap could reply, a man came running and said, "Ramesh Babu, hurry up, the embankment has cracked at another place, too..."

And thus the campaign lasted the whole night till it was dawn. The rain, at last, abated. The danger had now passed and Ramesh ordered his men to go home and rest. Only Ramesh and Deap remained there, resting their backs against the wet sandbags.

"Well, Mr. Deap Kumar, you must have got rich material for your films." The jealousy which had been suppressed by the excitement of the emergency was now manifesting itself in bitter sarcasm.

But Deap was composed and calm. "There is no doubt about it, but I have learnt that life is even more interesting and dramatic than films."

"So this whole situation, I suppose, appears to you like an episode from a film. The hero and villain are both here," he spoke, directly looking into Deap's eyes. "Only the heroine is missing."

"Well, then, here comes the heroine too," replied Deap, who was facing the path across the rain-drenched fields. Ramesh turned around to see Usha wading through ankle-deep water, looking adorably ridiculous in his raincoat which was too long and too big for her. When she came nearer, they saw that she had a thermos flask slung over one shoulder, while in the other hand she carried a tin of biscuits.

"I have brought some tea for you two," she said with a cheerful smile. "After a whole night's drenching, you might catch a cold."

As she poured the tea into the cups, a gust of cold wind blew from the river, and Deap sneezed.

"First give it to him," said Ramesh. "Those delicate creatures from Bombay catch chills too easily." He was getting sadistic pleasure out of such sarcastic remarks.

After giving them tea and biscuits, Usha walked up to the edge of the embankment to look at the repaired damage. "So, it was quite a big breach. Lucky that you arrived in time, otherwise..."

Her sandals slipped on the muddy embankment and she fell with a splash into the fast-flowing current of the river.

"Usha!" Ramesh and Deap both cried out simultaneously and before Ramesh could say anything, Deap had jumped in the water.

Ramesh, who was an expert swimmer, ran down the riverbank, anticipating that Usha would be carried thither by the current. But the moment he jumped in, he knew that he would have to save not only Usha but also Deap. Indeed, Usha, who knew a little swimming, had managed to keep herself afloat, the only danger being that the current could carry her too far. But Deap obviously could not swim at all and was floundering helplessly. He had already gone down and come up once. Ramesh tried to help him first but the panic-stricken Deap clutched at him so desperately that both of them went down together. When they came up, Ramesh disentangled his right arm and gave a boxer's blow to Deap, who was instantaneously knocked unconscious. Usha, struggling to keep herself afloat, screamed when she saw this but then she understood, because Ramesh had firmly caught Deap by his long, wavy hair and was now dragging him along while swimming towards Usha. Her legs badly caught in the voluminous folds of the raincoat, she too was about to go down when Ramesh reached her, and the first thing he did was to give a powerful tug to the raincoat and release her from its tentacles. Then his strong right arm reached out to her. "Hold on to my hand, Usha, and try to swim towards the bank. I have to look after this idiot, too."

Even in that perilous moment, Usha could not help smiling when she saw Deap's unconscious pale face and remembered the comically helpless manner in which he was floundering a few moments ago. As she felt the powerful grip of Ramesh's strong tractor-driver-hands on her fingers, she knew that now she was in no danger, and that the storm had passed.

GANGOO

After seeing off Deap Kumar and his unit at the station, they were driving back to the farm in their jeep.

"Ramesh!" began Usha.

"*Hoon!* Yes."

"Have you forgiven me?"

"Why should I. The fault was mine."

"Yours?"

"Yes. Mine! I should have known that roses are as important in life as wheat."

"So?"

"So I have written to the government that we must have a cinema here for the farm-workers so that we can regularly see films, especially Deap Kumar's next film, *Naya Hindustan*, in which our own farm figures so prominently."

"And then?"

"This year when I get my annual vacation, I will not spend it in research."

"What will you do?"

"We shall both go to Bombay and among other things, go to Deap's studio to watch him shooting films. After all, he especially invited us."

"I am not much interested in this film business."

"But I am, I want to see Deap at work in his own surroundings. I feel he is not bad at all; he seems to be sincere about wanting to make films with a purpose. But every man has his own sphere of work beyond which he is bound to feel at sea—as poor Deap was floundering in the river when he gallantly jumped in to save you. I am sure if I was made to stand under those blinding lights before a movie camera and asked to act, I would faint with sheer nervousness. Do you know what he told me before the train started? He said, 'Ramesh, on your farm during those three weeks, I have learnt much about life. You will see glimpses of this understanding in my new films.' That's why I want to have a cinema on the farm and to see his films."

"Must you go on talking about that fellow?"

"Why, what's the matter? I thought you were a great admirer of his. Now what has he done or said to make you angry with him?"

"What does he think he is? He has the cheek to say to my very face 'Mrs. Ramesh Chandra, I'm afraid you are not very photogenic for films. Your nose is too short and your eyes are too big.' I feel like punching him on his long nose."

"Oh, that was it. Vanity, thy name is Woman!"

"I prefer his wife—she is so dignified and so cultured, and yet so devoted to him. She flew all the way from Bombay when she learnt he was down with a chill."

"I don't like the way she treats him. As if he was a baby. I wouldn't stand for that sort of patronising attitude from my wife!"

"Oh, wouldn't you? But I tell you she admires him, too. She asked me about the happenings of that stormy night and when I told her how he worked in that downpour, even risking his life, I could see in her eyes that she was mighty proud of him. I don't think she is going to patronise him now."

As Ramesh applied the brakes, with a jerk, the jeep came to a halt in front of their house. He helped Usha to get down and then led her to the back of the house. "Come, I will show you something."

"Show me—and then I will tell you something."

"Look there—your rose bushes! I wanted to show them to you only when they had blossomed. Now you can look at the flowers from your bedroom window."

The rose bushes were there but without a single flower. There was not even a rosebud.

"Who has stolen the flowers? Ramesh was quite indignant.

"I did." It was Gangoo, and as he came out from behind the mulberry tree, they could see him laden with roses—red and pink and white.

"Please excuse me, Ramesh Babu, you were not here, so I picked them without your permission. You see... The fact is… Today I'm getting married, you see... But if you are angry, I will return them to you."

"No, no, Gangoo," Usha reassured him. "Take all the flowers and give them to your bride as a present from us. And remember, when you set up your own home, take some cuttings from here and plant a little rose garden of your own."

"Yes, of course. Thank you, thank you, now may I really take all these flowers?"

"Yes, certainly," Ramesh assented, "But give me just one rose." And he selected a big red one.

Gangoo went away, happy and buoyant, walking on air.

"Did you see?" Usha said, "Gangoo also adores roses."

"Yes," he agreed, "but do you know how much wheat he helps to grow with his tractor? It is only after one has grown enough wheat that one can appreciate the roses. Did you see how happy he is today?"

"He has reason to be. He is marrying Gori, the most beautiful girl in the village."

"Not more beautiful than the girl I love!"

"Ask Gangoo."

"Ask me." And saying this, he put the flower in her hair and lightly kissed the lobe of her ear. "Now tell me what you were going to say."

"It is only to be whispered."

"You are sure?"

She nodded.

"A sweet little Usha for us!"

"No, a naughty little Ramesh!"

"Look, Usha, there..." And as she turned, she saw on a bush the tiniest little rosebud, pink and tender, smiling at them like a newborn baby.

The "Fraud" of Film Festivals

(For Basu Bhattacharya)

When I met Zingaro at a film festival in North Italy, I was immediately struck by his handsome dark looks and his tall bearing. He looked like a younger version of Paul Robeson.

"My name is Zingaro," he said, introducing himself, "Perhaps you have heard of me as the director of *Drops of Oil,* made for my government last year."

I said I had not the privilege of knowing his work, but would watch it with interest when it was shown at the festival. "When is it scheduled?"

"On the last day of the festival" he replied, "Unfortunately the name of my country is Zamzam, so alphabetically it comes last."

He spoke fluent English but a little haltingly as if he did not have much practice.

"Did you *only* direct it?" I asked, wanting to know if he was also the writer, since it was a festival of author films.

"I did practically everything in the film—I wrote the screenplay, directed it, edited it and also played a small part in it. You know, I borrowed the idea from the late, great Alfred Hitchcock."

After this dining room conversation, we were seated at the same table. As my delegation consisted of only one man, and since he, too, was a single delegate and needed an English interpreter, a pretty signorina—educated in America and full of Hollywood gossip—joined us. Zingaro was obviously struck by her and tried his best to impress her with his importance in the film world. "I was invited to Cannes, but I preferred this festival as it is an Author Film Festival."

He also provided other details of his personal life to Signorina Pauline Passarini, with me included as an unwilling listener.

"My father is an oil tycoon—the oil gushes out of the oilfields and gold flows into our home. But my father is a practising Socialist and gives the highest wages to oil workers in the world. The moment a child is born in the family of one of his workers, his upbringing and education is undertaken by my father."

"This film was a gift—a birthday present—given to me by my father. He said, 'Zingaro, make a film that will bring glory to you, to your father, to your country.'"

I was interested in the country and took one of my Italian friends to the local library to look up Zamzam. This is what I read in the *Encyclopedia Britannica*. "Zamzam is the name of a British protectorate in the Mediterranean. It is a small island—about 100 square miles in area—with a population of only 13,457. The people were mostly desert bedouins but since the discovery of oil in the region, the country has flourished. Today it has the highest standard of living of any Sheikhdom in the Mediterranean or the Arab-Persian Gulf. The ruler is the Sheikh of Zamzam, a rugged old chieftain who is enlightened enough to have built schools and hospitals for his oil workers and for the British technicians working in the oilfields. Fifty per cent of the millions of dollars that he gets as royalty from the oil company, he spends on the welfare of his people. He has also built two cinema houses, one in the capital and another in one of the more populous oases where mostly American and Western films are shown. He has recently also laid the foundation of a local film industry..."

So that was Zamzam and its film industry, evidently given to Zingaro to play with.

He was not less than 25, but he had a child's naiveté and charming innocence. Even his pompous talk about his artistic greatness had an innocent quality about it. When he said, for instance, "If you ever come to Zamzam, I will come to receive you in my father's Rolls Royce," we had to believe it, for no-one could tell such a *big* lie. But when he said that his wife was expecting for the first time and was sure to have twins—one boy and one girl—one had to take it with a pinch of salt. When on the subject of his wife, he was apt to grow lyrical, though Signorina Passarina did not like it much. He would say, "My wife—she is more beautiful than any Hollywood or Italian actress. Coppola offered her a starring role when he met her when we happened to be in Hollywood."

"Why did you go to Hollywood?" I asked him.

"Because my film was nominated for an Oscar as the Best Foreign Film. That's why we had to be there, but ultimately a Russian film won the Award and I said, 'Let them have it, I am going to win a lot of awards.'"

But the festival was coming to a close, and the turn of Zingaro's *Drops of Oil* had not yet come. At least I was most anxious to see it to find out whether it had any of the qualities that its maker had attributed to it.

The day of the awards presentation came and there was still no sign of Zingaro's film. Five pictures were left to be shown on Monday and Tuesday but as the Chief Guest was available only on Sunday and he had to come from Rome, so the awards were already decided and all the remaining five pictures—including Zingaro's *Drops of Oil*—were given certificates of merit. Zingaro was obviously not pleased. It was not the certificate or the citation—which was in Italian and he could not translate it for his people—but what really annoyed him was that his name was misspelt as "Dingano" and his country as "Zomdom". After the director of the festival promised him that he would change the certificate on the following day, Zingaro was back in his element.

The next day, Zingaro's *Drops of Oil* was screened, and I was the most avid spectator. Since he was sitting next to me, I asked him why the writer-director's name was written as "Omar Khattabi" and he immediately retorted, "That is my assumed name. In our little country, there is a lot of jealousy. So I prefer to give my real name only in *acting* and always in the end, the way you end the picture with the title 'THE BEGINNING', and then comes your own title as Writer-Director-Producer."

And truly enough, when the list of actors came, it was arranged in alphabetical order: from Abdul Salam to Zingaro, which came in the end.

It was a small role that he had played—the young oil worker who brings the news of the first oil well gushing out oil to his king. But he played it with real aplomb, and it was apparent that he was the harbinger of glad tidings. He ran to the king, shouting in Arabic "Oil! Oil! Your Majesty, oil has been found."

That was all. His role was finished with the cameo of an appearance.

"How did you like it?" he asked me in a whisper.

I wanted to say it was "all right" but I didn't want to dampen his enthusiasm, so said, "It was *great.*" "I am glad you liked it," he said, "The king himself was pleased with my performance. He, too, used your words—*it is great.*"

The film, as a first effort, was quite good—a combination of documentary and story-film. It was made in a Neo-Realistic tradition, and that was why Italians generally liked it. There were questions and answers at the end.

"Who is the director?" one critic asked.

"I am the director," replied Zingaro.

"Liar," I thought to myself.

"Who is the producer?" was the next question.

"I am the producer though I have not taken that credit. I have given it to my company—Shirkatul Cinema Zamzam."

"Lying again," I thought, but I liked his gumption.

"What do you want to say through this film?"

"I want to thank Allah, the Beneficent, for giving us oil. I want to communicate the excitement and the pleasure it brought to my people who were living like nomadic beggars before oil was discovered. That is why I have chosen the smallest role in the film because the message of the film is in it!"

"He certainly has a glib tongue," I muttered under my breath.

"Come along to my country and see Zamzam," he said at the dining table that night. "Be my father's guest."

I said something about prior shooting commitments in Bombay. "Next time," I said, and got out of the embarrassing situation.

That was in 1977. The next year, I met him at Tashkent. He had come with the same film. He spoke with the same over-confidence. He had the same facile, glib tongue. Here there were no festival prizes. But he got a prize from the "Oil workers of Uzbekistan"—a silver replica of an oil derrick!

I parted with him at the Tashkent airport, where he was holding forth to a Russian director about his alleged forthcoming co-production—*Fraud*. I said to myself, "The fraud of film festivals."

But that was not the end of the "Fraud".

I met him again at the Algiers Film Festival. I was really stunned by his shrewdness and cunning in carrying the same film from one festival to another. "What about your new film?" I asked.

"It is going to be a co-production with Mosfilm Studio, and the Moscow people need time for preparations. It is going to be about the Soviet assistance to the Arab world and will be called *Tale of True Friendship*."

That night, at the dining table, when he repeated the invitation to me to come along and be his guest in Zamzam, I asked him how long it took to fly out there.

"From here we go to Rome, and from Rome airport it is but a two-hour non-stop hop."

"Then I will come. When do we go?"

"Tomorrow. I must arrange your ticket."

I was sure the ticket would not arrive. But to my surprise it did—and a First Class ticket it was.

We rode in an Alitalia plane in the—at least for me—unfamiliar luxury of First Class.

"The Zamzam Air plane is tomorrow," he said, "But why wait?"

Exactly after two hours, a speck appeared in the sea. When we came lower and approached it, the outlines of a palm-fringed island came into view. Rising above the palms were the oil-derricks.

The formalities at the airport were dispensed with.

There was no interrogation by Immigration officials, neither for me, nor for any other passenger—European and Arab—who got down from the plane.

There was no Customs inspection.

"Why spend a lot of money on maintaining Immigration and Customs officials?" he spoke with new authority.

There was the Rolls Royce waiting for us—just as he had said—driven by a *burnoosh*-ed Arab. He drove recklessly through the oil derricks that seemed to surround the airport and then proceeded along a straight metalled road through the desert. The road ended in a grove of olive and palm trees, amidst which was set what looked like an Arabian Nights palace.

"Where are we going? Is that the Desert Hilton?"

"No, it is the king's palace. You are his guest."

"I did not know that!" I confessed. But at least the mystery of the Rolls Royce was solved.

The sheikh received us with true Arab hospitality and warmth. He kissed Zingaro on both cheeks and shook my hand effusively. Then he said something in Arabic to Zingaro which I did not understand.

"Did you get a prize at the Film Festival?" he said in fluent English.

"Yes, father, I did," and he produced the colourful parchment which certified in French that *Drops of Oil* was one of the entries at the Algiers Film Festival.

Then the sheikh said to me, "You must be tired after the flight and would like to rest in your apartment."

I said, "Thank you, Sir" —and I accompanied an Arab servant down the corridor to a luxuriously furnished suite of rooms with a bathroom the size of a normal bedroom, with a green marble sunken bathtub.

I revelled in this unfamiliar luxury, wondering all the time whether Zingaro was indeed the spoilt son of the sheikh, who had his father's fortune to strut about with at the film festivals.

I chose a moment to speak to the sheikh about it at the dining table on which only the two of us were present—Zingaro had not yet arrived. "He has gone to see his mother, probably," the sheikh explained.

"Are you not spoiling your son by giving him so much money to go to all these film festivals?"

"*My* son?" He repeated, then he said, "*All* the people of Zamzam are *my sons*. That is what the sheikh is—a father to all his people. As for the money that is given to him for going to the festivals, it is one morning's earnings from the oil wells and, with it, he is doing excellent PR work which is bringing results, dividends. In fact, do you know three years ago, after the British left us, no-one had heard of Zamzam; today, we are members of the United Nations. Both Russia and America have opened their embassies in our capital. Now both are vying for our favours and offering competitive prices for our oil."

"Zingaro—but the name is not Arab. Why does he call himself Zingaro?" I asked.

"That you better ask him. He told me that Abdel Fateh—which is his real name—was too prosaic a name; Zingaro would attract attention at the film festivals. Also, it had an affinity with Zamzam, the name of his country and mine. So he got my permission to change his name."

"What is his background?" I asked out of curiosity.

"He is an orphan. He has no father except me. So I look after him like a son, as I look after all the fatherless children among my people. In childhood, he saw a 16mm film show in the palace. Since then, he was fascinated by the medium. He got an 8 mm camera, then a 16mm camera, experimented with films, till he bought the 35mm equipment—which I got for him and for the Shirkatul Cinema Zamzam, the Zamzam Cinema Co-operative. At last, one day, he made a film and showed it to me, and said he would take it to the festivals. You know, we have no lack of money or foreign exchange, so I thought it would be a good idea if he would take *Drops of Oil* to all the festivals as a Public Relations job to familiarise the world with the name of Zamzam. Since then, he has been everywhere—even to your India—and we are establishing commercial relations with every country where he has gone with the film. That's what you call his background."

The sheikh paused after the long speech and puffed at his cigarette, which was in a gold cigarette-holder.

"Where did he learn all the languages?" I asked him further, and that's when Zingaro joined us.

"Forgive me, father, for being late," he said, "A new print of *Drops of Oil* has arrived from the laboratory in Rome and I was checking it. But now I could answer our Indian friend's question."

"Go ahead," ordered the Sheikh.

Zingaro turned to me. "I learnt English—or you might say 'American'—from the American oil workers, as I learnt Russian from the Soviet oil workers."

I accompanied Zingaro on a tour of the whole island—the oil-derricks, the airport, the Palace and its galleries, the old Arab town and villages, the new colonies of pre-fabricated modern bungalows for the people who were still in the process of shifting from the old town with its squalor, the Hospital and the School. I learnt that the revenue from oil was so much that the Sheikh did not know what to do with it. So he promulgated a law that every male child born in Zamzam was to be given an educational subsidy of 5,000 dinars (1,50,000 rupees in Indian currency) and every girl-child would get an educational subsidy of 3,000 dinars and another 2,000 dinars at the time of her marriage. Every oil-worker who came in from America would get 5,000 dollars gratuity from the Government of Zamzam when he went home, and every Russian oil-worker would get 5,000 roubles when he departed to Azerbaijan or wherever he came from in the Soviet Union.

Now only one mystery remained to be solved—the young lady who was wife to Zingaro, who was supposed to be as beautiful as any Hollywood film star, whom Coppola wanted to cast in his film.

So, I asked him on the last evening of my stay, "Are you not going to introduce me to your wife?"

"Wife? What wife? I am not married yet," he burst out. "Come over to my house and you will find no trace of female company."

Then he took me to a comfortable air-conditioned bungalow near enough to the Palace so that the Sheikh could send for him at any time.

There were festival awards and framed certificates on the walls, on cinema, its history and technique, all over the house; there were dozens of shirts, jeans and jackets hanging in two wardrobes, and also white and black Arab costumes. But there was no trace of a young woman reputed to be more beautiful than any Hollywood film star.

"But you told me yourself that your wife is as beautiful as any Italian or American film star!" I felt like a child being cheated of a toy.

"I must have mixed up the *tenses*—I meant that I propose to have such a wife, and do you know, with my father's help, I will get whatever I want."

I didn't believe he had mixed up the tenses. After all, most of the things he had said were substantially true.

I last saw him waving me goodbye at the Zamzam airport. His last words were, "See you at the Moscow Film Festival or maybe at Cannes next year."

As I looked out of the window next to my seat in the comfortable Zamzam Air Boeing plane, I saw him waving to me, a dark, slim boyish figure, who had once learnt to play with an 8mm camera.

Soon our plane lifted off from the runway, and that figure was lost in the oil derricks, the palms and the olive trees that surrounded the island.

Saturday Night Fever!

(For Uma Vasudev)

The fever had come from the United States of America.

But, like an epidemic—an answer to Asian 'Flu?—it had caught on all over the world, including India, especially Bombay.

Sunita had caught it the first time she saw the John Travolta film. The handsome young man in tight-fitting trousers by his frankly sensuous dance movements did things to her, and to the other girls who confessed it to her later, that he sent a shiver all over their bodies, especially in the pelvic region. Each forward thrust of his body was felt by Sunita as a personal—and pleasurable—attack on her vicariously but physically. And it was set to a pulsating rhythm which seemed to be contagious, as most of the audience—consisting of teenage boys and girls who seemed to move up and down—were affected. Not since the advent of Rock 'n Roll had such a phenomenon occurred in Bombay.

In the darkened auditorium, Sunita had abandoned herself to dreaming of the American youth whose dancing had a subtle, sensuous, magical quality, and, fantasising amorous relations with him, she imagined herself to be in his arms, swaying to the rhythmic music in place of the ageing professional dancehall partners—the next moment, she was the other girl whom he was chasing, and dancing and matching her body movements with his thrusts and withdrawals, separate from him but joined to him by the music and the dance, and the sexuality they both represented. But the girl on the screen had no make-up. To Sunita, she was not worthy of Travolta. On top of it, she was a snob. Sunita enjoyed it when he called her a "sleazy whore".

She, Sunita, fancied herself to be in her place.

In school, she had loved poetry—Wordsworth, Keats and Shelley—but she had never *seen* poetry. Now she was seeing poetry in the body and the movements of Travolta.

But what was that? In the dark, she could feel a male body stirring towards her. It was her neighbour to the left. Now his rough coat was touching her left elbow. She knew the gambit as a well-known "pass"! The man's right knee was also touching her knee. There was some sensuous thrill in that touch which a sophisticated play-girl like her would not have minded; she might even have welcomed it as a male's tribute to her own femininity. But the moment belonged to Travolta and any other male was unwelcome at that moment. She squirmed in her seat to avoid contact with her neighbour to the left, only to brush her bare right shoulder against the person on the right, between the two of whom she was sandwiched. She wanted to be alone with the handsome young man on the screen but here she was given a seat between two males, both of whom, in the sensuous atmosphere generated by the picture, were anxious to have a brush with her body, howsoever small and insignificant the contact might be. Since a tall Arab, with his scarf tied to his head, was sitting ahead of her, she had to lean to the left or the right to keep her eyes on the screen.

The neighbour to the right seemed to misunderstand her squirming and moving in her seat, and took advantage of her involuntary touch by leaning on her bare right shoulder. He was wearing one of those new-fangled sleeveless T-shirts which were suddenly in vogue with 'he-men' those days and, therefore, his touch had much more direct—and naked—meaning than the rough jacket on her left. So she let the touch continue without readjusting her position. He mistook it as tacit consent and, a little later, she could feel a rough and callous hand expertly but gently stroking her bare elbow. So she decided to make most of the moment. The fantasy with Travolta was now physically complete. The touch on her shoulder and elbow was the Travolta touch—it was as if the delectable shadow on the screen had magically extended his hand to touch her body. She had seen the picture already three times, and so the music was enough to tell her that he was dancing. She closed her eyes to enjoy the contact with the man's horny head.

Before the picture ended and the lights came on, she felt an envelope being thrust into her hand. She had no time even to see the face of her "lover" of the darkened auditorium, for he had already turned away and was leading a plain-looking not-so-young woman—doubtless, his *wife*, she contemptuously thought! So she kept the envelope in her handbag and, adjusting her sari-end that had slipped from her shoulder, she followed the crowd streaming out of the balcony, clattering down on her high-heeled "mules" down the marble stairs.

Soon, she was in a taxi, going "home" to her paying-guest accommodation with a Christian family in Byculla.

In the taxi, as there was no light, she could not inspect the envelope. So, leaning back in her seat, she started dreaming of Travolta and also a little of the man in a sleeveless T-shirt.

After reaching home and having dinner with the landlady's family, when she went to her own room, she opened the envelope and found a card in it. It was not a visiting card but an invitation card to a film star's birthday party the next day—it was a Saturday—at a bungalow in the Juhu-Vile Parle Development Scheme. There was a name written on the envelope—"Mr. Marco Polo, the Maker of Stars"—with an address in Warden Road.

It was her dream come true. For the last two years, she had been "struggling" to get into movies, she had got herself photographed in black-and-white and in colour, the photographers had chosen her poses, taken liberties with her and convinced her to put on low-cut see-through blouses and off-shoulder saris till she had been photographed (more than once) in the nude altogether. But she had discreetly covered her face with her lustrous black hair so when the photograph appeared on the centre-spread of a naughty "magazine for males", very few who were not aware of her anatomy, including her family, away in the Punjab, had recognised her.

That had led her to modelling assignments, several so-called producers had "interviewed" her, approved of her good looks, declared her to be photogenic, taken her for drinks, dinners and dances. She had thought that the high road to film fame and fortune lay through the hotel rooms of the "producers". She had taken the plunge, been tested and tasted by a whole range of "producers" and directors but the only thing she got out of that was

"I Was A Maiden Once"! The costly gamble had failed. She was still a "struggler", struggling to get into the movies which seemed an unending and far-off dream.

This invitation card, therefore, looked to her like the magic lamp of Alladin. At last she had the breakthrough that she had longed for, had aspired and yearned for. Tomorrow, she would put on one of her most fancy and daring costumes which were lavishly bestowed on her because of her modelling assignments; she would perm and perfume herself with the headiest and sexiest perfume, and she would drive down to the party like Cinderella. She knew her Prince Charming would be waiting there for her!

Marco Polo (if that was his real name—Sunita had her doubts) was waiting near the entrance to save any embarrassment to Sunita. He was now dressed, Travolta-style, in a white suit with tight trousers tucked into ankle-length black boots. In this natty outfit, it was difficult to guess his age. His pomaded hair was jet black. But Sunita speculated that he must be nearing 40. "You look simply *à la grande*!" he commented on Sunita's dress and coiffure, which had startled him. For, she was dressed in a yellow see-through maxi which had wide flares and accentuated her slim waist. Putting his arm round her midriff, he led her to the bar while greeting the celebrities he passed.

"Hi, Dharam," to Dharmendra.

"Hi, Marco."

"Hi, darling,"—this to Parveen Babi.

"Hi, Marco. Introduce us to your girlfriend."

"Hi, Amit"—to the tall Amitabh Bachchan.

"Marco, Marco," a tall, young star hailed him, "Can I have an appointment with you tomorrow?"

"For you, any time, *yaar*."

Sunita was dizzy with the names she heard. It was "Hello, Dilip Saheb" and "Hello, Raj Saheb"—the only two senior stars to whom Marco deferred and to whom he showed some respect. Otherwise, it was "Hi, Ronoo," and "Hi, Dabboo" and "Hi, Chintoo."

Near the bar was standing the legendary IS Johar, "Hi, Johar Saheb", he greeted him.

"Hello, Marco," said Johar, while his eyes were riveted on the upper anatomy of Sunita, visible thanks to the see-through maxi.

"How would your friend like to appear in my next TV film?"

Marco was quick to reply before Sunita had a chance to speak. "She will be most glad, but not tonight."

With that, he gave a broad wink to Johar which was reciprocated though not appreciated.

When Johar had sauntered away, casting backward glances at Sunita, Marco ordered the barman, "Give us two Patiala pegs each." When Sunita raised her eyebrows at Marco's "tall" order. He explained, "It's very very boring to come back again and again for a second and third peg, so I believe in ordering a Patiala straight away, and then *chhutti* (relief) for at least one hour." He took a big preliminary sip from his glass, but cautioned her, "Go as slow as you like, daahrling."

Sunita, the sophisticated "struggler", did not want to seem a greenhorn at such parties, and only laughed at Marco's suggestion. She matched her first sip with the man who was escorting her (whatever his real name was), not forgetting to say "cheers" as she clinked glasses, reminding him what he had to do in the first place.

A fiery two-edged knife slid throughdown her throat, but she swallowed it, maintaining an air hostess-like smile on her lips. One had to be prepared for these occupational hazards when aspiring for quick stardom.

Returning from the bar, they were waylaid by a fat and ugly man in a crumpled suit, whom Sunita instantly recognised as one of the minor producers to whom she was once introduced. It was the early part of her "struggle" and he had dismissed her in two minutes with the usual formula of "Leave your photographs with our production manager. We'll call you when we need you." Twelve months had passed and she had not received a call from the producer. But tonight, as he looked at her, a vague bell rang in his memory. When had he seen her before? Was she the call girl whom his friends from Delhi had sent? Or was she only a model whose photograph he had seen in the paper, or on the TV? He was already drunk, and his speech was faltering. "Hello, Marcosh. Have I seen your *farend sumwhere*?"

"No, Sir," Sunita said very firmly, "You and I don't move in the same circles." She gulped down the drink to restrain her anger, and then gripping Marco's hand firmly, she sauntered away.

"I don't like this *haramzada* (bastard), always poking his nose in other people's affairs. Putting on airs just to impress you. Hasn't paid my bill for the last two months!"

"What bill?" Sunita asked herself silently.

Sunita was so provoked to see this producer who had once rejected her that she accepted another drink and took a big sip. Now it no longer felt like a knife going down her throat.

Meanwhile, music started somewhere, which seemed strangely familiar. It was the opening strain of the *Saturday Night Fever* cassette. Sunita's hips responded to the music, compulsively. "Shall we dance?" suggested Macro.

"Yes, why not?" she hissed back, but she said it to Travolta, rather than to the pomaded Marcos (or whatever his real name was).

In the garden, trees were festooned with multi-coloured lights and the tennis court had been converted into a dance floor. "Fever Disco" was blazing in neon lights and the lights all around the tennis court went crazily on and off. You could not see clearly who was dancing with whom. Nor did anybody care. There were at least three young stars dressed, like Marco, in Travolta's white suit. Sunita started dancing with Marco, who was a fairly good dancer. But among the four Travoltas, there was one who had not only the good looks but also the vivacity of Travolta, and soon Sunita was dancing with him. The lights went on and off, blinking and winking. The new Travolta was an expert in disco dancing, he knew all the Travolta steps, as did Sunita—so the two were very well-matched and tried to synchronise the movements of their bodies. He thrust his tightly-trousered middle portion forward, she retreated, then it was her turn to thrust her pelvis forward, and his turn to retreat.

The Patiala peg was making Sunita's head spin, but she was enjoying it too, as if watching the whole drama from outside of herself.

It seemed to her like a ballet in which she was the heroine and John Travolta was the dashing hero. She did not know the name of this particular imitation-Travolta;

she only knew he was young and handsome in a hungry-looking way.

When the tune slackened and they were dancing close to each other, he paid her a compliment. "You dance very well. But I haven't seen you around. What's your name?"

"Lovelina—that's my name," Sunita lied, but she had decided that when she became a star, that's what she would like to be called, "You dance very well yourself. What's your name? Do you know all these people?"

The rhythm was pulsating now and the mood of the dance had changed for a faster beat. The boy's answer came in spasms, "Thank you," he said, thrusting his body forward.

"My name is Tonny Travolta," he said retreating, subtly, beating the air with both his hands.

"Just a coincidence," he lied without conviction.

"I am just a struggler,"—then he put his hand on her shoulder and whispered in her ears, "Actually, I am a gate-crasher here—just a junior dancer for the present. If you like, we could make a pair—just us!"

Sunita reacted as if stung by a viper. She thought he was a star on the upgrade, and she would climb up, like a creeper, by clinging to him. That he was himself a "struggler" came as a big blow to her. And a gate-crasher at that! What cheek! She had half a mind to report to the host that here was a gate-crasher whom she had caught red-handed. Then she remembered that she was herself a gate-crasher of sorts, she had not been invited personally either, but was only the un-named "friend" of Marco Polo, who had not even bothered to introduce her to the host.

The moment she thought of Marco, she saw him dancing the tango with a plump starlet who was gasping to keep pace with him. Sunita cold-bloodedly abandoned her partner of nearly an hour and went to relieve the exhausted plump girl.

"Oh, hello," Marco was evidently glad to be rid of the starlet, and to be joined in the dance with his original "date", but there was visible complaint in his voice as he said to her above the music from the blaring loudspeakers, "Where have you been, *daahrling*?"

Sunita shouted back, "Well, I have been dancing with this or that,"—and she mentioned some names which might impress him, for they were present in the crowded medley of the dancers—"but," she added, "most of the time I have been searching for you. But there are so many men in white suits that it is difficult in this tricky light to distinguish one from the other."

It was only then that Sunita saw that Marco had been dancing with a half-full glass of whisky on his head. Pointing to it, he said, "I put on a show so that you could spot me."

"Oh, Marco! That was really clever *and* sweet of you. How stupid of me not to have noticed you."

"Never mind," he said at her contrite confession. "Let's get out of here. It's nearly one o'clock."

"All right," said Sunita, but without enthusiasm, for she had been greedily eying the buffet tables where dinner was being served while there was a lull in *Saturday Night Fever*! The blaring loudspeakers were suddenly muted and there was an enormous noise because of 500 voices simultaneously talking.

"Let's go somewhere we can have a quiet talk. You can also eat what you like."

He escorted her to the exit, where a long, sleek, red imported car was waiting with a uniformed chauffeur.

While they made themselves comfortable in the plush-covered back seat, the driver skillfully manoeuvred the limousine out of the jam-packed parking lot and then drove to Hotel Ripples, which was not far away from Juhu beach. The receptionist recognised Marco, saluted him and handed over the keys to his room.

"You live in this hotel?" Sunita ventured to ask in the lift.

"No, but I keep this room for my special clients and come here when I want to have a quiet talk with them."

When the door opened into the drawing room of the suite, Sunita found the walls literally covered with portraits of the most famous stars and upcoming starlets, each inscribed "with love" or "with gratitude", "yours sincerely" or even "yours affectionately".

"Did you *make* all these stars?" she asked.

"They call me 'The Star-Maker'. But I don't claim to be that," he said with genuine modesty. "They have got talent and photogenic features, and I help them acquire a star personality."

"Marco!"

"You know that's not my name. They just call me Marco Polo."

"Why?"

"Because the real Marco Polo discovered many new countries and continents. I discover—and invent—the stars and even planets."

The doorbell tinkled and a bearer entered with a wheeled table loaded with chicken sandwiches, *tandoori* (roasted) chicken, and a bottle of champagne. "Whenever there is a film-land party, I prefer to eat here," he said, producing a ten-rupee note with which he tipped and dismissed the waiter.

While sipping her second glass of champagne, Sunita hesitantly asked, "You have made so many stars. Do you think I can make the grade?"

He did not give an immediate reply. He looked hard at her, got up, adjusted the table lamp so as to let the light fall full on her face, adjusted her hair, and only then declared, "Yes, I think you have got a very good chance. You have quite a star personality, you know. Just a matter of clipping off some hair to give you the 'Sadhna Fringe'."

Sunita had had a big dose of whisky, and also two full glasses of champagne. But this "compliment" proved to be the headiest of all. Her head seemed to swirl. The lights were revolving. She tried to steady herself with a bite of a sandwich.

She looked at Marco. He seemed like the Prince Charming who would take Cinderella in her gilded coach to the fabled tower of the Castle of Success. Her heart went out to him in a surge of love and gratitude. She approached him and held his face between the palms of her hands. Then she kissed him full on the cheeks, which were smelling of an after-shave lotion. There was a faint click of a switch and the lights went off. Cinderella felt herself carried to the gilded coach by the strong arms of Prince Charming.

The sun was streaming through the windows when Sunita opened her eyes. She looked at her watch. It was past 10.

Where was she? Were all the events of the previous night a delicious dream induced by *Saturday Night Fever*?

She was certainly not in her plain and oddly-furnished room in Mrs. De Costa's boarding house. She seemed to have slept in a double-bed in a hotel bedroom. She looked about for some sign of the person with whom she had shared the double-bed.

Beyond the crumpled sheets and blankets, stood someone who oddly resembled John Travolta in a white suit. But he had, beneath his mop of hair, *no eyes*! She went up to it and discovered it was a clothes hanger on which a white suit was hanging with a Travolta wig on top of it. That had, in her champagne-sagged mind, completed the Travolta image! But it was only a white suit—*and a wig*! Was that Travolta? Just a tight white suit and a wig of hair? Then it flashed across her awakening mind. If the man had used the wig, he must have been bald. Now she remembered snatches of last night's conversation.

"Hasn't paid my bill for two months…"

"My special client…"

"Just a matter of clipping off some hair and giving you a 'Sadhna Fringe…'"

She rummaged through the drawer of the dressing table.

She found a couple of cards among the photographs of stars and starlets, with and without their wigs and hair-dos, and, on the card, read: "Marco Polo, the Star-Maker—HAIR-STYLIST AND WIG-MAKER." In one corner was an address of a beauty clinic c/o a five-star hotel in the Fort area. In the other corner was an address on Warden Road—the same address that was on the invitation card envelope.

Impatiently, she rang the bell.

The waiter entered, carrying a letter on a tray which he presented to her.

"Pehalwan Saheb has gone to work and left this for you."

"What name did you say? What Saheb?"

"Masita Pehalwan Saheb—this is his room!"

Masita Pehalwan—or Marco Polo? They were one and the same.

She opened the envelope. From it slipped five hundred-rupee notes. Also, a card of Marco Polo's. On the back of the card was written, in a childish scrawl: "My dear, God—by for present. But come to my Beyuty Clinic when you went wid or widout *apoyntmant*. I shall give you new *parsonaliti*—and also more letters of *introduction* to producers who are my clients. Thank you for everything. Yours, MASITA."

Thicker Than Water

Ever since he moved into our locality, strange things were being whispered about him.

One said, "Must be a runaway convict who had broken jail. That's why he keeps so much to himself, never meets anyone, never talks even to his neighbours."

Another would remember, "It's three months he's been here and no one so much as knows his name!"

Still another would advance his theory, "The poor fellow is obviously suffering from an incurable disease. Don't you see the strange pallor on his face—as if there is not a drop of blood in his veins? Must be TB, if you ask me. That's why perhaps he keeps away from others, to avoid spreading the contagion."

But another would contradict this theory, "Sick, indeed! Have you ever seen him bringing a bottle of medicine?" Then he would dramatically drop his voice and whisper, "I tell you…a CID man, a police informer. If he was himself a criminal, *they* would have caught him a long time ago. After all, he comes and goes in broad daylight. But no one has ever seen him doing any work. Then where does he get the money to pay rent and buy his food? From the police, of course!"

That line of reasoning was unquestionable. It was quite true that he had no ostensible means of livelihood. For days, he did not stir out of his room. Then one day, early in the morning, he would emerge like a frightened rat, he would softly put up the latch and lock his door, taking elaborate care not to make a noise, then he would slip out of the lane, walking with quick steps, with his head bowed down. Usually, he returned by noontime, now walking slowly, as if he'd had a stroke of a mysterious sickness. Once, we even saw him stumbling along, as if he was drunk, supporting himself against the wall of the lane. But he was not drunk. There was a strange pallor on his face and his deep-sunken eyes proclaimed not the wild flush of an alcoholic but the hopeless despair of a man condemned to an incurable disease. Every time he returned, he carried a cloth bag bulging with flour, rice, pulses, salt and oil which he would buy from the grocer's shop on the main road just outside our lane. He always paid cash for whatever he bought, the grocer had testified; he had never asked for credit. Without doing any regular work, how did he get all that money? This was the mystery which all of us in that locality were curious to unravel.

One day, when most of us were clustered around the solitary communal tap in the *basti*, we saw him coming down the lane. As usual, he was carrying his bag of provisions. He looked particularly fatigued that day. His old, patched-up shoes were coated with a thick layer of dust. His lips looked dry and chapped...and strangely bloodless. As he moved slowly, supporting himself against the wall, we noticed that his legs were wobbly. He took a few unsteady steps and then he collapsed. When we ran to help him, he was unconscious. Two of us lifted him, the third picked up the bag. The bottle of linseed oil was broken and an oily film was already spreading over the stagnant water of the gutter.

As we put him down in front of his door, he recovered his consciousness. Blinking his narrow and deep-sunken eyes, with a trembling hand he fumbled in his pockets and handed over the key. A powerful whiff of musty and stale air assailed our nostrils when the door was opened. Inside, it was dark as if neither light nor air had ever penetrated here, like a cave. No, like a vaulted tomb! Harbans, the ice-cream seller, turned away with a look of an unknown fear on his face. So did Govind, the scooter driver. Holding his nose, he went and spat out in the gutter. Only Saxena, who was a proofreader in a press, remained to lend his shoulder to his nameless neighbour, who somehow hobbled to his cot in a corner. Saxena pushed open the small window in the rear of the room and blinked at the sudden intrusion of light. Everything was in confusion and disorder. On the loose-hanging cot strung with coir-rope lay a threadbare and mangy blanket and some rags which served as bedding. Unwashed utensils lay near the *chulha,* hearth, in one corner. A pile of coal and ashes, half-burnt faggots, rotten vegetables and onion peelings—everything stank with an odour of decay… and death! Saxena, having glanced round the room, now looked at the man on the cot, who was trying to get up but evidently finding the effort too much for his strength.

"What's your name, brother?" Saxena asked casually to start some sort of conversation, and was quite unprepared for the brusque and bitter reply he got.

"What's it to you?"

"Well...er...I just asked," Saxena, taken aback, blurted in confusion, "I was only trying to be of some help. You are quite sick you know. Maybe we should take you to the hospital."

"I am not sick," the man spoke in a voice which was weak but strangely firm and determined. "Who says I am sick? You want to cheat me of my livelihood? You want to kick me in my stomach?"

Saxena decided the man was under some sort of hallucination. Maybe it's the fever, he thought. Then, trying to change the topic, he asked, "Brother, why do you live alone?"

"Because there is *no one!*" The man sighed after a pause. "Want to ask any more questions?"

"Yes, what do you do for a living?"

From deep down the hollow chest came a gurgle which could be a chuckle or a spasm of dry cough, or both, and then he said. "Where is the work that one can do for a living? I am on the waiting list in the Employment Exchange, but a thousand registered before me must get jobs before I get one. To drive a scooter, one must have a license. For the license, you need money. Where is the money? Where is the job? What am I doing?" Again, his mind seemed to be drifting.

He must be a criminal, Saxena thought. Maybe a pickpocket? Or, who knows, some kind of pimp? Maybe a dealer in narcotics. He decided to ask a final question: "So, what exactly do you do?"

For a moment, there was a strange flicker in those dull, dead eyes, as if he was about to utter a grim sort of joke, "I...I...I deal in..." Then he seemed to change his mind and remained silent. But Saxena followed the look in his eyes which came to rest on a dark, blackish-red spot on the sleeve of his dirty shirt. It was blood. Fresh blood! In a sudden burst of panic, Saxena fled from the room, followed by that ominous ring of hollow and humourless laughter.

The next day, when he went to work, he was haunted by phantom spots of blood floating on the proof sheets before him. On his way home, he edged suspiciously away from anyone who stood near him in the bus. He felt the blades of unseen daggers tickling his ribs. Back in the *basti,* as he passed the house of the nameless stranger, he found it locked from inside. It remained locked the next day...and the next...*and* the next! And all those nights, Saxena could not sleep, he was tense and jumpy till his nagging wife could endure it no longer and burst out. "What is the matter with you, man? You look as if you have committed a murder!" The next morning, it was still dark when Saxena slipped out of his house.

We were all queuing up at the water tap when police van arrived. Four constables, a sub-inspector and...Saxena!

He led them straight to the door, which was still locked from inside. A few kicks of the policemen's boots and it burst open with a tearing of rotten wood. This time, too, a whiff of stale air escaped from the room. Saxena groped his way to the window, and the room was flooded with the slanting rays of the morning sun.

The man lay inert on the loose-hanging cot. The blood on the shirt had now dried up into thick black spots. The sub-inspector touched the arm that hung over the side. The body was cold and lifeless.

"He has been dead for some time. There will have to be a post-mortem."

But there was really no need for a post-mortem. Not far from the dead body lay a heap of creased and yellowing papers. The sub-inspector picked and read them, one by one:

"Irwin Hospital, Delhi. 21st January 1961. Ramlal, son of Shamlal. Paid Rs. 10."

"Municipal Hospital, Delhi. 5th May 1961. Mohammed Baksh. Paid Rs.10."

"Government Hospital, Rohtak. 7th June 1961. John Lewis. Paid Rs. 10."

"Irwin Hospital Blood Bank, New Delhi. Chhotu Ram son of Ghasita. 11th July 1961. Paid Rs. 10."

There were dozens of such chits but up to the end, we could not know what his real name was. Among the papers was also a much-creased old clipping from some newspaper, with an article about the "life-saving blood bank" and a photograph of several people in a queue to donate their blood...and, among them, the man who lay there, dead, in clothes spattered with his own blood!

Saxena took the clipping from the officer and read: "Doctors operating the blood banks in Delhi hospitals have revealed that some unemployed and impecunious people are habitually selling their blood to make a living. One such man, under different aliases, has traded his blood more than 30 or 40 times. A doctor told our reporter that such frequent blood-donations can prove fatal to the donor..."

An Evening in Paris

CUSTOMERS of Wide World Travel Agency—among them some of the most seasoned globe-girdlers, both Indian and foreign—never failed to appreciate and commend the spick and span appearance and ultra-modern décor of its offices which matched, as it were, the courteous efficiency and phenomenal resourcefulness of the organisation. The pastel blue walls were covered with murals done by a Ceylonese painter, known among the smaller and more exclusive art coteries of Bombay and Colombo as the "daring young man with the flying brush". These paintings, which bore eloquent testimony to what could only be described as the "aeronautical sweep" of the artist's brushstrokes, represented a colourful but somewhat crazily mixed cross-section of the wide world to which the travel agency offered the golden key—for the price of a plane or steamer ticket, of course! The Eiffel Tower seemed to have replaced one of the minarets of the Taj Mahal, the Pantheon stood cheek by jowl with the mud huts of the Mexican *paisanos*, while bubbling liquid from giant-sized champagne glasses were overflowing into the lotus-covered Dal Lake!

The gleaming steel furniture, the glasstop tables, the map of the world in plaster bas-relief which covered one entire wall of the outer office, the discreet concealed lighting, the thick, spongy, deep blue carpet on the floor, the frosted glass partitions which enclosed the cubicles of the top executives—in short, everything bespake the good taste and aesthetic sense of Mohan Vaswani, the Managing Director of Wide World Travel Agency, Ltd. The younger son of a Sindhi millionaire, he had acquired a flair for travel in his father's far-flung chain of silk stores (which extended all the way from Colombo through Hong Kong, to Tokyo and even Vancouver) and an arty-crafty veneer during the six months of a hectic holiday in the Latin Quarter of Paris.

Yes, the customers of Wide World found in the offices of their favourite travel agency, every fascinating incentive to titillate their jaded and, in many cases, sated appetite for foreign travel. The colourful pictures, the exotic decorations, the miniature Eiffel Towers, the soapstone Taj Mahals in glass cases, the Lilliputian skyscrapers of New York, the clipped Americanised accents of the smartly dressed assistants who looked after the requirements of the tourists at the various counters—everything was designed to conjure the exotic and the romantic. Everything—except one!

The plain-featured, dark-complexioned Kamla Kamtekar, who had lately been appointed receptionist, was the only ungainly, even ugly, spot in the otherwise impeccably elegant surroundings of Wide World. Invariably clad in a home-washed white cotton sari, her flat hair coiled in a bun and reeking of coconut oil, she conjured not the exotic visions of Montmarte or Manhattan but only the odorous bylanes of Poona or Satara or some other unknown small town in Maharashtra.

The sophisticates in shark-skin suits who frequented the offices of Wide World were not only disappointed but quite taken aback to be confronted with this 'Plain Jane' at the receptionist's desk. Some of them who were on more intimate terms with the Managing Director, even voiced their dissatisfaction with his latest choice which, they pointed out, was not only incongruous in a smart establishment like Wide World, but also militated against the firm's hitherto unbroken tradition of smart, good-looking and glamorously groomed receptionists.

"That's just the point," Mohan Vaswani would point out to his disgruntled customers. "A receptionist like that is, undoubtedly, an ornamental decoration for the office, but look at the trouble it causes me. Every few months, by the time I have trained a new receptionist—and you know that this job calls for something more than just good looks, a receptionist in a travel agency must have the whole wide world at her fingertips—so, I was saying, by the time a new receptionist has been sufficiently trained to be of practical use to the office, someone from among you chaps comes along and falls in love with her, and the next thing I know is that she is handing in her resignation along with an invitation to a wedding reception. "Remember Kitty Kilawala," Mohan would go on to illustrate his point, "the young socialite who created a minor sensation in Bombay society when she joined us? Before we could teach her that punting is a popular river sport in England and not a town in China and that the Comet and Constellation are types of planes used in international flights and not astral phenomena, she had gone and got married to Bobby Bhukhanwala, the heir to the Bhukhanwala millions, whose itinerary she had completely messed up by reserving his seat on a steamer to Genoa in Italy while he wanted to fly to Geneva in Switzerland for winter sports. When he missed the plane by which he had intended to leave, he came storming into our office demanding to know what kind of a fool had upset his plans. Kitty was so sweet in her apologies that Bobby left after 'dating' her for dinner and dance that very evening! The next week, the society papers announced their engagement.

"Then there was Maya Gupta, the Bengali beauty with those famous eyes who came to us after three years in Oxford, where she was known to be a minor poetess and a budding playwright. She was not even a month with us when she was 'hooked' by 'Sonny' Sharma, the famous tennis champion and sports editor of the 'News', who came to our office to book his passage to Helsinki but changed his mind after meeting our pretty receptionist and, instead of covering the Olympics, left two weeks later on a honeymoon trip to Kashmir.

"The loss of Asha Mathani—you remember she used to be Miss Karachi before Partition—is, of course, too fresh in your memory to need reiteration, but the defection of Diana Collins, the Goanese dame with the figure of Venus, who eloped with an American businessman who had just casually dropped in at our office to encash a traveller's cheque, was the last straw that broke the camel's back. From then on, I decided, no more pretty receptionists for Wide World!"

And so the plain Miss Kamla Kamtekar, B.A. (Honours in Geography), with her home-washed cotton saris and her plaited hair coiled in a bun and reeking of coconut oil, her sallow, dark complexion unrelieved by powder or rouge, her thin lips unadorned by lipstick, and her beady, short-sighted eyes blinking self-consciously behind the thick lenses of a pair of cheap, steel-rimmed spectacles, had walked into the shoes of her glamorous predecessors.

Within a week, she had impressed her new bosses with her efficiency. Her knowledge of Geography was a distinct advantage in a place where names of outlandish foreign places—Kamachetka and Buenos Aires and Yokohama—were always being bandied about. She lost no time in committing to memory all the relevant information sought by would-be tourists. In time, she became a talking encyclopaedia of international travel—she knew the exact distance between San Francisco and Los Angeles, or from Yokohama to Nagasaki, the airfare from New York to Rio de Janeiro, and she could map a safari through the darkest Africa in less time than anyone else could take to locate London on a large-scale map of Great Britain.

The intricacies of foreign currency and exchange were at her fingertips, so that she could work out orally how many dollars and cents could be exchanged for a thousand rupees or a thousand roubles or a thousand kronins! And, in course of time, even the most fastidious clients of Wide World came to appreciate her efficiency and to trust her judgment in planning their detailed itineraries. They, poor souls, knew that the Wide World's new receptionist was a little hard on the eyes but they also knew that she would never give them the wrong tickets!

Kamla, who had been a school teacher—her special subject being Geography, of course—before she joined Wide World, brought to bear a pedagogic thoroughness to her new job and also a patronisingly maternal interest in the client's welfare. "I hope, Mr. Moolji, you are taking plenty of warm underwear. The English weather can be treacherously cold in early spring", or, "You should, by all means, take your child's perambulator with you, Mrs. Saksena. There will be plenty of space for it to be wheeled around on the promenade deck." She would caution one against confidence-tricksters on the Trans-Atlantic luxury liners and advise another on the sights worth seeing in Rome.

To a young student travelling to London via Paris, she would issue the maternal warning, "Now, remember, young man, if you must break your journey in Paris, the things to see are the Louvre museum and the palaces of Versailles or if you like, the UNESCO headquarters. Don't you go about wasting your time and your parents' hard-earned money on sampling the sinful nightlife of Montmatre," while to a grey-haired diplomat off to Lake Success for a UN Session, she would offer, along with the ticket, her hopes that the Indian delegation would exert the growing prestige of India in the cause of world peace, and to a film star bound for Venice to attend the International Film Festival, she would say, "You are going just in time. De Sica's new film is being released in Italy this month."

Sometimes a client, stumped by her uncanny knowledge of foreign places, would ask, "How do you know all this, Miss Kamtekar? Have you been there?" And Kamla would answer with a sigh, "Oh, no, Sir, I have had no such luck, yet." In the unconscious emphasis that she invariably gave to her "yet" was the sum total of all her secret aspirations and yearnings of a whole lifetime.

For underneath her plain, schoolmarmish, even forbidding exterior, Kamla was an incurable romanticist.

Ever since the first Geography lessons she had learnt in primary school, she had wanted to go abroad, to visit the exotic places she had read about, and to experience the kind of romantic adventures and escapades she had read of in certain kinds of English novels and American magazines. For a lower middle-class, small-town girl who had to go through school and then college with free-ships and scholarships, tuitions and part-time work in a rationing office in Poona, even to come to Bombay was an adventure. To go abroad, leisurely in an ocean liner, or swiftly by air, all this belonged to the realm of dreams. The receptionist's desk in the Wide World Travel Agency was the nearest she had come to the realisation of her secret ambitions.

And yet she was full of dreams, so that every evening when she took the crowded local train from Churchgate to Dadar, it might have been the "wagon list" across Europe, and the walk to her chawl through the narrow slum alleys was an adventure into the Limehouse area of London or a ramble through the ancient cobbled streets of Paris. The miniature model of a Skymaster which stood on her desk took her on a different flight every evening—to Cairo or Rome or London or New York—when she was always the last to leave the office. But her favourite dream flight was to Paris which, in her imagination, was composed of the novels of Victor Hugo, Dumas and Zola, the short stories of Maupassant, and the numerous illustrated folders issued by the French Tourist Department with which their office was so liberally stocked.

She knew these were dreams, but she also knew that dreams, sometimes, have an uncanny habit of coming true. So, in the strictest secrecy, she had taken certain precautions against being caught unawares in a moment of lucky emergency. Locked in the lowest drawer of her desk was a passport—she had applied for it within a week of joining Wide World—and also a certificate of inoculation against cholera, typhus and yellow fever, as required by international health regulations. She had this certificate renewed every three months, the momentary pain and discomfort of the injections being a small price for a precious dream. One day, someday, her chance would come, and when it came, she wanted to be ready to fly to Paris if necessary at a moment's notice!

It came sooner than she could ever imagine and, one evening, out of the blue heavens as it were, dropped into her hands—a ticket to Paris by that very night's plane. It was the hour after closing time, when daily she stayed behind in that vast office to sort out the pile of correspondence—a twilightish moment of suspended reality, when, like timid but venturesome creatures, her dreams were wont to emerge from the pile of folders and pamphlets and coupons and vouchers and waybills and reservation slips that lay cluttered on her desk and went soaring to all points of the compass marked on the relief map on the wall.

So when first she saw it, she could hardly believe her eyes and, for a moment, thought it was but another dream. Yet there it was, the crinkling paper real to the touch: a return ticket to Paris issued by a world famous international airline in the name of—believe it or not—Miss Kamla Kamtekar, valid for the outward flight of that very date, the plane scheduled to take off from Juhu airport at midnight.

The ticket was real enough—not the figment of a dream. Moreover, Kamla knew how the miracle had come to pass. It was an unusual sequence of coincidences but none of them, by itself, was impossible. It was in the nature of things that a fabulously famous and rich film star like Devibala (her last film, *Kali Naar,* had been a golden jubilee hit) should take it into her head to fly to Paris for a holiday. It was in keeping with the mystic rituals of the film industry, that she should seek to shun publicity by travelling incognito under an assumed name—maybe it was a case of 'purposeful modesty', the aim being to exploit this anonymity for later publicity!

Whatever the reason, these stars had their little whims and fancies and they could certainly pay for them—the fact was that some days ago, Devibala had walked into the office of Wide World, bringing with her a whiff of some expensive foreign perfume and an air of exotic glamour all the way from the crown of her Ajantaesque hairdo to the lacquered toe-nails sticking out of the Greco-Roman sandals. She had confided to Kamla—"as one woman to another, my dear, and no third person should know anything about it"—that she proposed a two-week flying tour of France, Italy and Switzerland but most of the time, of course, she wanted to spend in Paris. "Gay Paree," she had pronounced it, in self-conscious simulation of the French accent.

"But," she had insisted, "I don't want any publicity, so I want to travel in toto."

"You mean 'incognito'?"

"Incognito, of course, that's what I mean. All these crowds of fans absolutely shatter my nerves. As one woman to another, you can appreciate my desire for a little privacy, at least for the brief period of this holiday."

As one woman to another? Kamla looked from the translucent chiffon sari, through which the star's brocade *choli* and powdered midriff were clearly visible, to her own home-washed cotton sari, but she readily agreed with the star's views on the need for privacy. She was already drawing up a provisional itinerary for the celebrated client, but all the time her heart was pounding out the bitter invocation, "Oh, why should it be her, why not me? Why not? Why not?"

And so it was but natural that when she asked Devibala under what pseudonym she would like to travel, and the mentally preoccupied star failed to think of any suitable name for herself and asked Kamla for a suggestion, she should have blurted out, "Why not Kamla Kamtekar? That's my name, you know."

Devibala had readily agreed to the suggestion and walked out, leaving a cheque to cover the price of the ticket which was duly purchased for her by Wide World. But then, on the very day that she was to leave, late in the evening, a few minutes after closing time, Devibala had rung up to say almost casually that she was cancelling the trip, adding something about some "dates" which she had to give to some producer to complete his picture which required a lot of "retakes" due to drastic "cutting" by the censors. Anxiously looking at the clock, Kamla had tried to explain on the phone that it was too late for cancellation, that the airline would not make a refund, that it would mean the dead loss of several thousand rupees. But the star had replied: "What are a few thousands when a few lakhs are involved?" and then abruptly rung off.

And now that very ticket was lying on the table—an exciting invitation to adventure, a challenge and an invocation, a dream and the answer to all her dreams. Would she dare? Could she dare?

Then the clock on the wall had begun to chime—one-two-three—the chimes sounded hollow and eerie in the deserted office—four-five—was she running a temperature or was it the excitement of the momentous decision she had to make?—six-seven-eight—why were the walls of the office going round? —nine-ten—then the chimes ceased with a whirl of the clock that was like the final warning of Time itself. It was now or never. NOW—or NEVER! Now? Never? Would she? Could she? All her hidden desires, her secret longings, her lifelong ambitions and aspirations were now rising within her in a burning fever of excitement, as the music of her blood rose to a crescendo merging into the mighty whirring of propellers—it was the miniature Skymaster on her table, or was it?

No, it was a giant skyliner, as real as life itself, and now she was on it, clutching her passport in one hand and the ticket in the other, easing herself into one of those luxuriously upholstered seats about which she had read so much in the airlines publicity blurbs. The smiling air hostess—she, too, seemed to have walked out of an advertisement—was now telling them to fasten seat belts, please. The next moment they were off—the illuminated map of Bombay, diamonds studded on black velvet, was going down and away, finally sinking into the dark and fathomless ocean of the night.

The air journey proved to be exactly as she had so often described in detail to would-be air travellers to France—early morning in Cairo, flying over the Pyramids (from that height, they looked ridiculously like little toys floating gently in the waves of the desert), then on to Rome and over the ruined shell of the Colosseum (just like the photographs) till at last, sparkling in the afternoon, Paris itself came spinning up from the earth: the slim cone of the Eiffel Tower, Notre Dame with its castle-like battlements, the domed Opera House, the tree-lined boulevards and, cutting through them like a long, straight knife, the Champs Elysees, and then, coming down, down, down to Le Bourget airport!

PARIS, Paris, Paris at last—Paris, the city to which her most daring dreams had led! And here she was in Paris, no longer in her dreams, but really, truly, physically there.

"Taxi, Madame?" The taxi-driver tipped his cap, opening the door of the cab with elaborate courtesy and to Kamla, his face, too, seemed to be familiar—was he out of a movie, or a book, or a dream?

"Où allez-vous, Madame?"

"À *l'hotel*," she said, briefly, too self-conscious to try out her college-acquired French, then she added, "Hotel Champs Elysees," and that name, too, was out of a dream—or was it out of the list from which she had been recommending hotels to the clients of Wide World coming to Paris?

The hotel, too, was a dream—a dream conjured up in marble and mahogany and gilt-framed glass, with a wide, sweeping staircase and a tiny toy of a lift which, of course, was not called a lift here but an *escalier*.

And her room? It was more like a movie set of Marie Antoinette—with an enormous gilded four-poster bed and heavy brocade draperies. The glow of the sunset was in the sky, and the gay hum of the boulevards was in the air, an invitation to stroll out. This was no time to be locked up in a room, even so gorgeous a room as this one.

A hot bath in the blue porcelain tub was welcome after the tiring journey, but as she stood wrapped in the soft, fleecy towel, a disturbing thought stung her. Could she face her first—and who knew, it might be the last—evening in Paris, dressed in her home-washed cotton sari? Could she? With trembling hands, she opened her bag—but what was that? A couple of gorgeous bird-of-paradise saris and a velvet cape embroidered in gold! The dream dress of a fairy princess?

Could it be that her bag was somehow, somewhere, exchanged with someone else's, maybe with that of the young princess who was a fellow passenger on the plane? But this was no time to question a miracle or a lucky coincidence or whatever it was. It was time to be out on the boulevards, to savour the evening air of Paris, to seek romantic encounters or, maybe, adventures, to be seen, to be admired, to be courted and loved! But who would admire her, court her, love her? The thought of her ugliness pierced her with the sharpness of a rapier, and it was a despairing look that she cast on herself in the mirror.

She failed to recognise the image. If it was herself, something had happened to her, a strange transformation, for the face that looked at her was far from ugly, indeed, it had a dignified beauty of its own, and was enlivened, or rather, illuminated, with a smile. It could be that the joy of being in Paris had brought about the change in her looks, along with the change in her mood. It could be that this, too, was a miracle. It was her face, no doubt, but she had never seen it before—except in dreams!

And so when she came out of the hotel, she was not surprised to find admiring glances being cast at her. As she walked down the broad boulevard, many of those sitting in the pavement cafés, sipping wine or beer or coffee, forgot the glasses or cups in their hands, as they watched Kamla walk by, and once she caught the whispered comment: "*C'est une princesse indienne.*" She, Kamla Kamtekar, mistaken for a princess. "*C'est un rêve,*" she thought in French. "It must be a dream!"

And then, out of nowhere, it seemed, out of a dream, as it were, walked the handsomest young man she could ever imagine, even more handsome than Charles Boyer, to whom he bore a certain resemblance. She had to drink hard to remember her French lessons to understand what he was saying.

"*Permettez-moi de me presenter?* May I introduce myself, Mademoiselle?"

She nodded nervously, taking the seat he gallantly offered her, and as he himself sat down beside her, he said, "I am Count Paul Emile Verdoux," a strange and yet familiar name, but she was too excited to worry where she had heard it before.

"*C'est un plaisir, Mademoiselle,*" he said. "It is a pleasure, a very great pleasure to show you round Paris. *Garçon,*" he called out to the waiter and ordered champagne and as the bottle was brought wrapped in a napkin and placed in a silver bucket of crushed ice—just as in the movies—it took Kamla a few moments to realise that there was no prohibition in Paris.

"How did you know I was coming?" she asked in her broken, trembling French.

"I always knew you would come. I have been waiting for this day all my life—waiting and dreaming of it."

"So you too have been, er, dreaming of...?"

"Yes, I have been dreaming of you."

"And I have been dreaming of you!" she confessed, overcoming her shyness and, for the first time, looking into his eyes.

"So let's drink to ourselves and to this meeting, which is like the sweetest dream that two people ever dreamt together!"

She sipped the champagne—as she had seen being done in the movies—and then he raised her hand to his lips and imprinted on it a warm, soft kiss that sent waves of happiness tingling all through her body.

He suggested that they walk down to the Arc de Triomphe, which now stood perfectly silhouetted against the softly pinkish twilight. Arm in arm, they walked—and to Kamla it was the realisation of all her dreams: Paris and the Count, but the Count was the personification of Paris, handsome, gallant, cultured to his manicured fingertips. And brave, too, for as they neared the Arch, a roguishly rakish young man whistled when he saw Kamla and winked at her in a manner that had only vulgar implications.

Within the twinkling of an eye, the Count had challenged the man to a duel, and both had mysteriously produced rapiers from out of the folds of their dresses, and before she could realise what was happening, her beloved Count was fighting a duel—to vindicate her honour!

A few people had by then gathered to watch the duel, but none of them cared to interfere with the two swordsmen, while Kamla stood petrified by the swift and dangerous turn of events.

The rapiers clashed and flashed in the dimming light as the swordsmen parried and thrust, thrust and parried—just as in the movies—but then the Count made a swift stroke which sent the other man's rapier flying in the air and as the steel blade came clattering on the pavement, the Count's rapier had pierced his opponent's heart. With a vicious thud, the heavy body came down, and Kamla could see blood on the Count's blade as it was withdrawn.

The Count made a deep bow. "All for you, my dear," he said. But just then, a whistle sounded in the eerie stillness of the evening. Police!

"Gendarmes!" the Count exclaimed and, all of a sudden, strangely forgetting all about the fair one for whom he had fought the prohibited duel, he ran down a side street, with Kamla desperately racing to catch up with him.

Through narrow lanes, and narrow bylanes, ancient cobbled alleyways, she ran and ran and ran panting for breath, close behind the fleet-footed Count but never exactly catching up with him, as he went around a corner and disappeared—forever! The police whistled to urge her onwards, she ran and ran, till in a blind alley she came to a staircase and ran up wildly to hide herself before the gendarmes caught up with her. Then she slipped and fell, hitting her head on the stairs…and all was dark and dreamless night.

When she woke up, she was lying on the cot in her room and the girl who shared it with her, a Third Year medical student, told her that she had slipped on the stairs and fractured her skull, and had been lying in a state of delirium for two days and two nights. "It was the most peculiar delirium I have known, for you were all the time talking of Paris and some Count whom you wanted to catch and bring back to your office. 'I will keep the Count in a glass case, he will be good publicity for Wide World.' That's what you were saying over and over again. You better get yourself psychoanalysed."

"How was I dressed? Did I have something with me?" Kamla asked weakly, exhausted by the shock of awakening after such a hectic dream.

"You were dressed in the same old sari," her friend informed her, "but you had a plane ticket to Paris clutched tightly in your hand."

A few days later when she returned to office, the first thing Kamla did was to ring up the airline.

"This is Wide World. I am sorry I could not inform you in time but that return ticket we got from you for Miss Kamla Kamtekar has to be cancelled."

She could not believe her ears when she heard the reply that came from the other end over the wire.

"What? Will you say that again?" she screamed into the mouthpiece.

"We don't know what you mean by a cancellation. Kamla Kamtekar has already been to Paris and come back. She came to the airport and said she had lost the ticket, so we issued a duplicate. But do you know she spent only one evening in Paris? Some strange customers you send us sometimes."

And Kamla wondered if there was a dream within her dream, till the next day's movie columns in the papers came out with the story of how Devibala, the popular star, flew incognito all the way to Paris and spent only one evening there—returning immediately in response to an urgent call from her studio.

The Most Beautiful Woman In The World

The boy in narrow trousers and a loud Hawaiian bush-shirt, perched on his bulging hold-all, looked up from the newspaper and winked at his companion. "Look, man! Iona Pinto! Bombay girl who came second in the World Beauty Contest."

The other boy in a maroon T-shirt, who stood leaning against the door of the compartment, took the newspaper from his friend, looked hard at the portrait, and then puffed out a long streak of smoke aimed at the dimpled cheeks of the Beauty Queen. "What, man, I see many such girls every dance night at the Byculla Railway Institute."

Then they started talking about the girls they knew—Stella D'Souza who had a torso like Marilyn Monroe's Luc, a ChaCha champion, and Josie, who was plump but a real "sport" and laughed all the time…

And just behind the two Byculla blades, squeezed between the window and a fat Lalaji, I was thinking about the hard time the judges in a beauty contest must be having. How do they arrive at a decision? Is a girl beautiful because she can boast of a 38-24-38 figure? Who decides whether the black eyes of Miss Egypt are more beautiful than the blue eyes of Miss Iceland? How do they choose between raven tresses and flaxen blonde hair? What is the ideal complexion of a girl—snow-white, golden-brown, coffee and cream or ebony-black? Who is the more desirable girl—the tall, statuesque, athletic American in a bikini or the demure, petite, doll-like Japanese in a kimono? Do the beauty contests really exhaust the list of the world's beauties? I was sure there must be thousands of beauties who, like nameless roses, blush unseen in their own backyards. Who then, is really the world's most beautiful woman?

Whenever I am on a railway journey, my thoughts run faster than even an express train. Jammed in a corner of a third class compartment, I while away my time pondering over imponderable problems. Some of these questions I find provocatively peeping at me out of the pages of a newspaper, while other thoughts rise yeast-like from within myself. Who am I? What am I? And why? Whither are we going? Is the earth really round like the orange I have just peeled and thrown away because it was stale? Or is it flat like the *chapattis* (Indian bread) that I will be served for lunch at the next station? Whither is this earth moving? Towards any point, or is it just whirling round and round, aimlessly, spinning on its axis like a top? Whither is our country going? Viewed from the window of a running train, does it not seem that we are immobile while the land is running backwards? Maybe the whole world is in reverse gear!

Once again, I was lost in such thoughts when, suddenly, I became aware of the most beautiful woman in the world, sitting right there in that overcrowded Third Class compartment. For a moment, I wondered if she were not a figment of my imagination. Was I dreaming? I looked around to make sure of the crowded and, literally, pressing reality. My left arm was pressed against the window, and on my right hand the fat Lalaji was enthroned. Next to him sat his heavily-veiled wife, flanked by a whole series of their "editions"—the elder boy reading a children's magazine, the younger one trying to snatch it from him, and the daughter playing with her squeaking doll. The last in the line was a fat and dark "memsahib", who was constantly scolding Lalaji's daughter in her pidgin Hindustani. *"Arrey, baba, toom* naughty *nahin bano*. Straight *kambakth baitho*." (Don't be naughty. Sit straight.) Facing her sat a bearded Munshiji in a moth-eaten *sherwani* (long coat worn by men), sporting an equally moth-eaten kind of sparse beard. His wife, enveloped in a voluminous black burqa, and their seven children—the youngest of them on the mother's lap, and maybe the eighth one on the way—occupied the entire row of seats before me.

Behind them, by the window, was a sadhu with a long, bushy beard whose locks of grey hair were being ruffled by the wind. Next to him a youth, dressed in a suit straight from a small-town tailor with a shining imitation silk tie, a plastic rose in his button-hole, his hair carefully oiled and parted—obviously, on his way to an interview for a job or with his would-be father-in-law. Then there were three middle-aged men engrossed in a game of cards. And beyond them, a tall and rather slim young man pulling out a gleaming, stainless steel tiffin carrier from under the seat and handing it to her—his wife or his beloved? —the most beautiful woman in the whole wide world!

She was inspecting the food in the tiffin carrier and, sitting squeezed in my corner, I was staring at her. Never before had I seen such a beauty—neither among the film stars of Bombay nor among the fashionable socialites at New Delhi's diplomatic receptions, neither on the Bengali stage nor in the princely palaces of Rajasthan. But I could not analyse the elements of her beauty which made her so unique. Her complexion could not be called fair: it was wheatish-brown, but there was a glow on her unpowdered cheeks which was like the reflection from an unseen fire. Every time she raised her heavy, dark lashes to look at her companion, her almond-shaped eyes sparkled with an inner flame. Her half-open lips, untouched by lipstick, seemed to have tasted the most excruciating pleasure and the most tantalising pain of life. Her long, dark, shiny, plaited hair was set off by a single little red rosebud. She wore inexpensive, pain, pinkish glass bangles on her wrists and there was no ornament round her neck or on her arms. Under the edge of her sari I could see her delicate hennaed feet. In my life, I reflected, I have seen more shapely feet and slimmer ankles. I have seen more beautiful eyes. And yet why is the totality of her personality so uniquely fascinating? What is the secret of the unmatched beauty of this unknown girl in a crowded Third Class compartment?

They were now having their delicious meal, Fried *puris* (Indian bread), spicy vegetables and pickles that made my mouth water. With a loving, caressing insistence she was offering him more of everything and, with equal loving compliance, he was eating and relishing what she gave him. I imagined that she must have gotten up early that morning, with loving care she must have kneaded the flour and flattened the *puris* with the rolling pin, and then fried them in real ghee—for him to eat on their first trip together. The lingering, loving looks they gave each other made me think that they were newlyweds.

It must have been a love marriage, of course. Such tender love is seldom found in matches arranged by parents or professional marriage-brokers. I decided that they were on their honeymoon. The young man, with all sorts of economies and acts of self-denials, must have saved enough money to take his beloved bride to Bombay. There (I imagined) they will put up in some small, inexpensive hotel; with eyes full of love and wonder they will look at the great city from the top of double-decker buses. On their way to Juhu, and on the first thrilling glimpse of the sea, she will show him her gratitude with a silent loving glance. She will stand there on the beach, and the receding waves will play on her toes and she will experience a peculiar tickling, tingling sensation like the first caress of love. Then he will bay a tender coconut and offer her the milk and she will shake her head with a smile to suggest that he should have the first sip, and then the coconut will pass back and forth from the one to the other, and with the sweetness of the juice they will also savour the taste of each other's lips. Then he will toss the empty shell into the water but the waves will bring it back to the shore. This time he will throw it far into the sea, but after a while the shell will be back at their feet. Then she will begin to laugh for no particular reason in sheer happiness, and he will join in her laughter: they both will laugh and laugh till all the people on the beach will be turning round to look at them with much curiosity and a little envy. Someone will remark, "Look there, the most beautiful woman in the world!" And another will add, "There goes the luckiest man in the whole wide world!"

But they were still far from Juhu beach, having their meal in a crowded Third Class compartment. Now I saw that the world's luckiest young man was embarrassing his wife by feeding her like a child, putting morsels of food in her mouth. She was shyly but lovingly looking at him, and her face had turned crimson by the rush of blood to her cheeks, and in her eyes glowed the soft and sweet flame of love. Suddenly, like a flash of lightning, I was struck by the great revelation about the secret of her beauty. The secret was, indeed, no secret. It was love. Love! It was love that put that magical twinkle in her eyes, that glow on her cheeks like the reflection of a flaming fire, it was love that raised the yeast of youth to invest each part of her body with softness and sweetness of beauty.

The boy in the gay Hawaiian bush shirt who stood behind me looking at the Sunday newspaper was now pointing to another portrait: "Look, man, look at this photo of Miss USA who came first in the Beauty Competition. Most beautiful girl in whole world, man! I would give my right hand to have just one look at her."

I felt like shouting at them, "You fools, the world's most beautiful young woman is right here in this crowded compartment, seated only a few feet away from you, but you have no eyes to see her." But just then the train slowed down, rattling over the points, and soon it was running along the platform at Jhansi junction. I saw the fortunate young man getting down on the platform and I followed him to have a talk with him.

He stood, glancing around, searching for someone or something, perhaps the water-carrier, when I caught up with him and, without any introduction, straightaway asked him, "Excuse me, but are you going on your honeymoon?" There was such a noise and bustle and confusion on the platform, with porters hitting you in their mad rush with mountains of luggage precariously balanced on their beads, pedlars crying out their wares and beggars whining away for alms, that my voice was drowned in that medley of noises. He turned round and asked, "Ji, did you say something to me?"

"Yes," I now shouted, "I wanted to know if you are going on your honeymoon?"

"Oh!" he exclaimed with a look of surprise. "Whom are you talking about? We have been married for at least six years." He added with a smile, "We have left behind our four-year-old daughter with her grandmother." Then he said, "Please excuse me, but I must find the *dahi-vada* vendor." And he was lost in the crowd. The guard blew his whistle, waved his green flag, and passengers ran back to their compartments.

Back in my seat I glanced at her and noticed her anxiously looking out at the platform. There was a touch of beauty even in her look of anxiety. With a sudden shudder and loosening of the vacuum brakes, the train now began to move, and she involuntarily leaned forward, ready to jump down. Suddenly she caught sight of him and a smile lit up her face—a smile of such utter relief that I looked round and saw that he was already in the compartment carrying in a folded deaf the *dahi-vada*, dripping with the yellow spiced curds, and in his eyes was love and a look of triumph as if he was silently declaring,

"You asked for *dahi-vada* (Indian snack) and here it is. There is nothing in the worlds that I can't get for you."

Whenever there is a beauty contest, there are always articles in the newspapers by the contestants revealing the dietary secrets of their beauty. Miss England ascribes her lovely figure to a daily bowl of porridge. Miss USA recommends a glass of orange juice every morning. Miss France is partial to grapes and grape-wines. Miss Germany declares that to keep slim she lives on a diet of brown bread and skim-milk. But if I were asked what the most beautiful man in the world relishes most I would unhesitatingly answer, "*Dahi-vada*"—especially if her husband has had to jump into a moving train to bring the delicacy and to insist on feeding her with his own hand!

So the train thundered on through the vast expanse of the country. Soon it was dark outside and lights came on in the compartment which was now even more overcrowded than before. No one could even straighten his legs to sleep: we only wriggled in our seats now and then to fitfully doze for a few moments. But she was peacefully asleep, her head resting on her husband's loving shoulder. She was smiling even in her sleep as if she was having a sweet and happy dream. For a long time I kept on thinking about them and their love which was so fresh and so intense even after six years of married life. I decided that after reaching Bombay I would meet hem, invite them to my place, talk to them and find the secret of their uniquely perennial love. At last, even in my squeezed position, I too drifted into sleep, in spite of the fat Lalaji's snoring and the thunder of the train wheels and the song of the boy in the loud bush shirt, who was softly crooning something which I could hear only partially—"Darling, darling (something-something) I'm (something) dreaming of you."

And I dreamt that all the beauties of the world of all times were gathered for a beauty contest. There was Cleopatra of Egypt, Shirin of Iran, Laila of Arabia, Padmini of India, Josephine of France, Dante's Beatrice from Italy and England's Lady Godiva riding on a horse in her birthday suit. Blondes, brunettes, princesses, courtesans, real and imaginary beloveds of posts and the heroines of the world's great novels. And their lovers and admirers, like circus barkers, were shouting aloud to solicit support for their candidates.

"Vote for Cleopatra!"

"Shirin and only Shirin deserves your vote!"

"For superlative beauty, vote for Padmini!"

"Come, gentlemen, behold the matchless beauty of Lady Godiva..."

And in my dream I, too, shouted. "This is all nonsense. Come with me and see the world's most beautiful woman. She is right here in this Third Class compartment, sleeping on her husband's shoulder."

Then I woke up with a start and saw that it was daylight and the train was standing at Igatpuri station. But neither the world's most beautiful woman nor her husband was there. Their places had been taken by a couple of turbaned Maharashtrian peasants.

"Where did they get down—those two?" I asked the fat Lalaji and the bearded Munshiji.

The Munshiji spat out the remnants of last night's *paan* and replied, "I have just got up, *bhai*." Then he asked his wife, "Mother of Mohamdoo, did you see where they got down—that young man and his wife?" The veiled head silently shook to reply in negative.

The fat Lalaji roused his wife from her slumber. "Now, get up: soon we will be in Bombay." Then he turned to me. "Maybe they got down at this very station. Why don't you look for them on the platform? The train will stop here for quite some time."

I jumped down from the train, and there she was on the platform—the most beautiful woman in the world! No, this could not be that one. Her complexion was golden-brown, while this one was ebony-black.

But there was no doubt that this one, too, was the most beautiful woman in the world. She had the same sweet, contented smile of love fulfilled. Her lips, too, seemed to have savoured the most tantalising pain and the most excruciating pleasure of life. Her eyes, too, sparkled with love and happiness. Suckling at her satin-smooth black breast was her baby, and by her side sat on his haunches a long-haired, strongly-built, dark-complexioned youth smoking a *bidi* (Indian cigarette). All round them sat other labourers and their women and children with their spades and shovels and baskets, their pots, pans, bedding rolls and other belongings. They were obviously on their way somewhere to lay ain new railway line or to repair the existing track. And in their midst sat that black beauty, certainly a beautiful woman, feeding her baby at her breast, her eyes longingly, lovingly, caressing the bare, black, work-toughened body of her man. As she looked at him her lips parted in a beautiful smile, revealing sparkling white, even teeth. And in her face illuminated by love, and in her body moulded to perfection by nature and honest hard labour, I glimpsed a vision of beauty which I had never seen in a drawing-room, a film studio or in a club lounge.

"Where do you come from?" I asked them. At this intrusion of a stranger, the girl modestly covered the child at her breast, and the young man threw away his *bidi,* before replying, "From Andhra Pradesh."

"How long have you been married?"

"We're here in the jungle, laying this railway track, Babu, breaking stones the whole day long and sleeping on the station platform .Where is the time to get married, Babu? When we go home we will get the *pandit,* priest, and 'make' our marriage. Isn't that right?" And saying this he unabashedly looked at her, who was and was not his wife.

The engine gave a shrilll blast, the guard blew his whistle, and I ran to get into my compartment just as the train began to move. Form the window I looked back and saw that the dark young man was throwing his baby up in the air and the baby was laughing and the baby's mother was looking at both of them with pride and love.

Then the train went round a bend and that vision of beauty was lost. Now the overcrowded compartment seemed desolate. There was only the fat Lalaji and his heavily-veiled wife and the bearded Munshiji and his wife in the black burqa, and their seven children and, maybe, an eighth one, too, and.....

The boy in the narrow trousers and loud Hawaiian bush shirt was combing his wet hair and telling his companion in a voice charged with happy excitement, "This evening I'm going to take Stella to the pictures. You know Stella, don't you? Oh, boy, she's the most beautiful girl in the world!"

The Physiotherapist

Devendra Kumar was known in the film industry circles and the film press as the "Duper Star", because (as his own publicist had explained) too many had been called "Super Stars" or were claiming to be Super Stars. But there was only one Duper Star and that was Devendra Kumar.

"That face, distorted by pain, seems familiar," said the physiotherapist, Chitra Bhagwat, to herself when she entered the deluxe room in the Creak Brandy Hospital. There were flowers—bouquets and baskets left by producers, directors and fellow stars—everywhere. The room was simply reeking with the perfume of flowers.

Then, as she approached the bed, she recognised the face—she had seen it dozens of times on the screen, and hundreds of times on the covers of film magazines—with a shock not unmixed with pleasure. When she was sent to Room 144, she had expected the usual *seth* (businessman), more than the usual sheikh from one of the Gulf countries reeking of petro-dollars! She was told that the patient, who had a bad accident, had recovered from injuries but needed a few weeks of physiotherapy before he could be discharged.

"Mr. Kumar, I presume," she said with a sense of discovery and a smile that was not a contrived grimace, like that of an airhostess.

"You know me?" he asked her, feigning unnecessary surprise, for he was quite used to being recognised, even in a crowd.

"Who doesn't know you, Mr. Kumar? Tell me, how did the accident happen?" she said with her best bedside manner. She was still standing and trying to discover the reason for the pain on the handsome clean-shaven face that had launched several multi-crore motion pictures.

"I will tell you, but first please take a seat. I can't tell such a long story to a lady while she is standing."

She sat down on the edge of the only chair in the room, bending towards him so as not to miss anything that fell from those precious lips.

He recalled the story that he had told the reporters already dozens of times. He was doing a dangerous scene for which (he never failed to emphasise) any other Super Star would have engaged a "duplicate stuntman", but he believed in Realism with a capital R. So he had decided to have the rope tied round his waist and to be let down over the cliff, with a 2,000-feet chasm below. He had to climb the rope which the villain, much above him on the cliff-face, was supposed to be cutting with a sharp dagger. He had to make the perilous climb by holding the stiff and prickly coir rope with his bare hands, which had been badly lacerated in the process and, just as he was about to reach up to the cliff-edge, his blood-soaked hands had slipped on the stones and he had a fall which might have been fatal if the rope had given way under the weight. But he gave credit where it was due, to the man who was holding it on the hill above. But, still, he had a fall for about 50 feet, hitting his body against the stone ledges jutting out and receiving a severe concussion where he was tied to the rope. The result was that several ribs were fractured and there were deep wounds and cuts and bruises all over the body where the jagged edges of the stones had cut into his skin.

"But I survived, though rendered unconscious when they finally pulled me up by the same rope," he concluded.

"My God! That means you were providentially saved," remarked the physiotherapist. "Let me see your palms that bore the brunt of the injuries."

The Duper Star brought out his hands from their hiding place under the white hospital sheet that covered the blue blanket. They were fair, like most Punjabis', but they were hard and calloused like that of a farmer and though they bore healed injuries, the physiotherapist's trained eyes saw that they were injuries that had not been caused by a coir rope but by something else more pointed.

"Spread your fingers like this," she said and spread her own hand in front of him on the white sheet. She noticed her own coffee-coloured skin for the first time in contrast to the big fair hands that were lying there limp and folded. It needed the left hand to support it.

"I can't," he replied, "it hurts."

"Come, come," said the physiotherapist, "Try, at least. I will help you."

And she touched his hands, and tried to unfold them, gently. Her touch was soft and warm-blooded. It had in it a soothing sweet current of compassion too. She stroked the calloused hands with her own gentle and soft fingers. Slowly, Devendra's fingers relaxed under her healing touch and he tried to open them on his own.

"*Shabash! Shabash!* (Bravo!)" she urged him as if he was a child. "Just spread your fingers a little more."

"I can't...any further." He moaned. "It hurts like a sharp needle was inside, below the thumb."

"A sharp needle?" She stroked the thumb affectionately, but actually she was examining it clinically.

The Duper Star was perspiring with the pain though the physiotherapist's gentle and soft fingers had done much to lessen it.

Chitra Bhagwat gave a final caress to the Duper Star's palm and withdrew her hand. "We will begin the treatment tomorrow morning."

"Must you go?" gallantly he asked her, withdrawing both his hands under the blanket and the white sheet.

"Yes, I am afraid I must," said Chitra. "Today I came only to get acquainted."

Devendra looked about, trying to find some excuse to delay her. Then his eyes fell on the bouquets that were arranged on the side-board.

"Please take some flowers with you," he said.

"All right," Chitra said. One of the lessons that she was taught as a physiotherapist was never to say "No" to a sick person. But at the same time she knew the dangers of accepting expensive gifts from her patients.

She singled out a red rose and picked it out from the basket. "I will take just this flower. Thank you very much, Mr. Kumar."

In her flat sandals, she noiselessly moved away as the door of the air-conditioned room shut softly behind her, and Devendra was left with his own thoughts, and the two women in his life—his wife and his mistress who had been visiting him daily; the wife in the morning and the mistress in the evening. He had had hundreds of affairs in his life with all sorts of girls –film stars and vamps and extras, air hostesses, college girls and Lolita-type schoolgirls, even call girls and common prostitutes. But they had left no mark on his life. They had been casual one-day or one-night affairs, a few kisses stolen while occupying the driving seat in the privacy of his air-conditioned limousine, an hour or a couple of hours spent in a discreet hotel suite that he had maintained since his gay bachelor days, and then a quick goodbye kiss while he took her home, with requests to keep in touch from the girl's side—which, of course, he never did, never having any intention of continuing the liaison. He had an easy, friendly way with girls who "turned him on", but as far as possible, he never told them lies—he never told them that he loved them, he only told each of them that he found them *attractive* and *interesting;* would they care to spend a couple of hours with him, have lunch or a dinner date with him?

His manly charm was irresistible. But he had no feeling of male chauvinism, he never boasted about his conquests, but they certainly made him feel good, built up his personality, boosted his ego, and his image on the screen.

There were only two girls who refused his offer of a "date"—he married the first and, later, he "met" the second one, who was supposed to be a "maneater" of the Bombay film industry, who was doing a picture with him and was as notorious for her casual affairs as he was, but to Devendra, she deliberately played hard to get till not only had he to declare his love, but also pledge his undying lifelong devotion. And after that, she had not left him even for a single day—the night belonged to the wife; he always boasted that he went *home* daily to sleep, even if it was two hours after midnight. The wife used to wait for him like a *sati-savitri*, with food on the dining table. For a year after the marriage, this schedule was religiously kept, but when she found out about the other girl, and gave birth to their first male child, the nightly vigil was dropped at his own insistence. "My dear, you are a mother now and, at least for the sake of the child, you must look after yourself. It is important that you have your full night's sleep, and not wait for your film actor husband who has invariably double shifts." He left it to her imagination whether he meant double shifts in the studio or in bed, or both. But the wife understood and kept quiet.

The third female whose mere touch had so electrified him was this physiotherapist with magic in her fingers. She compelled attention not merely because she "turned him on"—but because the current that flowed into him from her gentle touch was not harmful like an electric current, but more like a painless injection of warm honey which he could feel entering his veins. He looked forward to her visit the next day with a heart thumping, like a schoolboy on his first romantic "date".

~

When Chitra came in the next morning, Mrs. Devendra Kumar was leaving. They met in the corridor and introduced themselves.

"You're Mrs. Kumar, I am sure," said the physiotherapist, recognising the sad-eyed, tall beauty whose photographs she had seen in all the film glossies. "Glad to meet you."

She extended her hand and the two hands met in a friendly greeting.

"Then you must be the physiotherapist Dev was talking about all the time," said the wife, who was also Devendra's distant cousin and had come to Bombay for a holiday when he first met her.

"Your touch is so gentle," said Daya (that was the wife's name) after their first handshake. "I am sure my husband is in safe hands."

"Of that I can assure you," said Chitra with a merry chuckle but she meant it in a different sense than it was originally implied by Mrs. Kumar.

Bidding goodbye to her new friend, Chitra entered Room No. 144.

"I have been waiting for you," grumbled the Duper Star like a spoilt, petulant child.

"I am sorry," said Chitra. "I was briefly detained by Mrs. Kumar in the corridor. I notice that you have already told her about me."

"Oh, *her.* Yes, I told her that I have a very intelligent and pretty physiotherapist."

"Mrs. Kumar is a most beautiful lady," said Chitra, "you are a lucky man to have such a wife."

"That's what they all say when they see her," he replied, but rather mournfully, as if he did not believe it. "When will you begin the treatment?"

Chitra Bhagwat seemed to be waiting for someone—or something—to arrive before she would start her treatment. She looked at the door that had slowly opened and a technician entered, followed by a wardboy wheeling in a portable X-ray machine.

"What's all this?" Devendra asked, looking at the equipment as it was put on the narrow table that was slid across the bed. An X-ray plate was put on the table in its protective metal case and Chitra asked her patient to bring out his right hand and place it on the plate. Reluctantly, Dev drew his right hand, again taking the help of the left hand to support it, as he put it on the X-ray plate.

"Spread your fingers," she said and helped him with the touch of her hand.

There was the click of the X-ray camera as he painfully spread the fingers. Then the equipment was wheeled out. The technician accompanying it said as he left, "The wet plate will be ready in five minutes."

In five minutes, Chitra brought the plate and showed it to Devendra. "Just as I suspected—there is a splinter of glass embedded under your right thumb. It will have to be taken out. How did a splinter of glass get on to that cliff you were climbing?"

"I am tired today," replied Devendra, sulkily. "Are you a physiotherapist or a private detective? When are you going to start the physiotherapy?"

"Right now, but only on your left hand, the right hand will have to wait for the surgical incision to heal. Bring out your left hand." And she went over to the other side of the bed to be near the affected limb.

"Hold my hand," she ordered.

Devendra unwillingly and carefully did as he was told. His grip had no strength in it but it was a pleasure to hold her hand.

"Hold tight!" she urged him.

He complied but when she pulled her hand away, the grip was too lax, and her hand easily slipped out through his fingers, like a warm and fluttering little dove.

"Try again," she said.

He again tried to adjust his fingers to hold her hand tightly in his grip. This time she had to exert herself a little more to get her hand released from the ex-farmer's calloused fingers. But she could feel there was revived strength in his fingers.

"Try again." This time it was he who spoke those words.

She slid her hand into his grip which was comparatively firmer now since the fingers had already been exercised. He held onto her hand desperately, exerting all his strength which was much depleted after the loss of blood and six weeks of hospitalisation.

"Hold it tight," she challenged.

And he gripped it with all his strength, which was considerable though diminished.

This time, she had to exert herself to release her hand.

Hand-holding, he had learnt, was the easiest and oldest overture to amorous interludes, and this hand-holding as part of physiotherapy was no exception. He was enjoying it as much.

But Chitra put an end to it after five times.

"Your grip is already better and stronger." She then suggested another "game". He was to hold together his five fingers in a conical fashion. She slipped in her index finger between the thumb and the rest of the four fingers. Then she forced her finger out of his closed fingers

The next time, he was prepared for the "game", and pressed his four fingers hard against the thumb. This time, she exerted herself to pull her finger out of the "trap", but she failed.

Again and again, she tried but his fingers had for years gripped the plough and the tractor-wheel on a farm in the Punjab; his hands had pulled out the heavy leather bucket from the irrigation well, and the fingers even of his left hand practised volleyball and *kabaddi*—the two rural sports in his younger days. He would not let the coffee-coloured soft finger of the Maharashtrian physiotherapist out of the trap formed by his five fingers.

After trying five times, Chitra abandoned the game.

"Now spread *your* fingers," she said gently, helping the process with her soft caress.

Urged by her words and even more by her soft touch, his hand relaxed and the fingers spread out and straightened themselves. She continued to caress the hand, smoothing out the wrinkles of pain. Because of five weeks of tight bandaging, the fingers had lost much of their elasticity and strength. Now, they were being revived. And as he alternatively closed his fingers in a fist and then spread them—the exercise she had demonstrated to him—he could feel a new energy and strength streaming into him. He knew that a woman's fingers could generate passion, but he never knew that they could work such miracles as well.

~

The next day, when the Duper Star was wheeled out on a stretcher trolley into the Operation Theatre, he was under the effect of a heavy tranquiliser, his mind was already befogged and in his ears was echoing the skeptical remark of the physiotherapist.

"How did a glass splinter get to that cliff edge you were climbing?"

"I am tired today," he had said to her, "but what are you, a physiotherapist or a private detective?"

The chloroform mask was applied to his face, and at once his mind floated away on a cloud of rose-pink haze.

His wife, Daya, was there, still beautiful but larger than life, dressed in a rose-pink nightgown, saying in a voice without rancour, but a voice that was cold and stinging, like the after-shave lotion in its irony, "Dev, will you please tell your girlfriend not to leave the hair of her red-coloured wig on the lapel of your coat?"

From far away came an echo of his own voice, "What do you mean by that silly remark?"

Daya, imperious with her royal airs, had said, "Darling, I have adjusted to your girlfriend. I don't mind if you have a dozen, the more the merrier. But what I object to is that she flaunts different coloured wigs on different occasions. Let her make up her mind—if she has one—what she would like to be: a blonde, brunette, or a redhead like the call girls in American movies."

Then the dream had dissolved into another dream when he was making love to Radha before the camera. It was a passionate moment when he embraced her and he could feel the quivering of her breasts under his pressure and that was clearly not in the script nor in the "guidelines" that the director had given them before the camera started rolling. It was a silent scene, filmed against the background of the scarlet sunset clouds. And he had whispered to her, "You are good enough to be eaten." He bit her ear and she closed her eyes in a spell of amorous ecstasy. Just then, his eyes fell on her red-haired wig. "Who advises you about the colour of your wigs? Surely not the art director!"

"Does it not 'turn you on', sweetie-pie?" she hissed back in his ear. She was still in the spell of her ecstasy.

"No, it has the opposite effect on me," he hissed back. "Surely you know what I mean?"

"Yes, I know, you bloody *zankha* (eunuch)! If the colour of my hair turns you *off*, then go back to that wife of yours with her dyed brunette hair and hide in her sari." She had raised her voice beyond the permissible range and the director had yelled, "Cut! Cut! No, no we shall try again." Then, lowering his voice, he had told them both, "This is not a realistic sex movie, remember, like *The Last Tango*. It's the usual Indian commercial movie, remember, where we don't and we can't forget the all-mighty censor." Then, he said something that had an immediate effect. "Now, the permissible passion, and no more." He further added, "You can be as vocal and passionate as you like in the car when you drive back to the Rest House."

They needed only this reminder to be *professional*, and while the sun was setting in technicolour in the background, they soberly and *professionally* enacted one of the tenderest love scenes ever filmed in India, which made them an incomparable Made-For-Each-Other Love Team.

Soon they were in her car, a sports model Toyota which she had acquired from a retiring Japanese diplomat. As usual, she was driving, and as usual, she was silent and well-behaved till she was on the hilly road out of the way of the rest of the cars. At the crossing, she swerved to the right.

"This is not the way to the Rest House," he warned her.

"It goes straight to the greatest Rest House where we shall always rest in peace," she told him between clenched teeth.

Then she stepped on the accelerator, and the car sped forward at an alarming speed.

"Your usual hysteria!" he remarked. "Look, I am sorry if I hurt your pride or your ego. I will take on the driving if you are not feeling well."

"No, I won't let you *drive* me. I am going to die and I will see that you die with me. I won't leave you for that frigid woman who is your wife. Till Death do us *part*."

"Radha!" In panic he yelled at her, "You stinking blackmailing bitch. You are mad, MAD, MAD! Ahead is the cliff-edge beyond which the road does not go." And he struggled to wrest the steering wheel from her hands. But she had the strength of a wounded tigress and wouldn't surrender the steering wheel. The car raced to its doom. But, as it approached the fatal cliff-edge, he managed to swerve the steering wheel and the car smashed into the trees at 60 miles per hour. In the last fatal moment, the gallant Devendra fell on Radha, protecting her, while the smashed windscreen splintered into tiny fragments, the tiniest one of which pierced the right hand of Devendra, the Duper Star.

They were both found unconscious, buried under a tree that had fallen on the smashed car, and the heavy body of Devendra, protectively lying over the unconscious, but otherwise, unharmed body of Radha.

The Duper Star had, indeed, acted out a heroic role in life which unfortunately the producer could not publicise. So he asked his Publicity Manager to suppress the car accident and give handouts to the press about injuries sustained in the cliff-hanging scene which had already been filmed without an incident or accident! So they invented the cliff "accident" to avoid the scandal about Radha and Devendra which would have ruined the reputation of both actors if the truth had leaked out!

~

When, after the small operation, Devendra opened his eyes and saw, as if through a haze that was no more rose-coloured, all the three women in his life—the wife Daya, the mistress Radha, and the physiotherapist Chitra—he did not want to confront all of them together, so he feigned unconsciousness again and closed his eyes.

But, now that they were all together, he had a chance to compare each with the other. Daya was, undoubtedly, the most beautiful of them all. She was also the most educated and cultured. But she was cold and statuesque, too intellectual to project a sexy image. Radha was all sex—passionate (especially in bed where all her acrobatic skills were concentrated)—and nothing else. Now that she stood beside Daya, she looked crude and vulgar.

Then there was Chitra, whom, already, he counted among the women in his life. Though he had known her only for three days, he liked her coffee-coloured complexion, her chiselled face with an upturned nose decorated with a little diamond-studded nose-ring. She had a quick intelligence—he still remembered how she had seen through his fictitious story about his hand lacerated by the friction of the coir rope! There was no nonsense about her. Still, her touch was friendly and warm; it had healing properties, not just a faucet which could be "turned on" or off. There was nothing crude about her, yet her touch indicated a reserve of emotional, sensuous power that could bring bliss to him, the one on whom it was bestowed. She was a combination of the good qualities of Daya and Radha without the weak points of either of them.

When he was well enough, he decided, he would see more of Chitra. He was tied to Daya by marriage vows, but he was through with Radha and her inordinate sexual demands. Perhaps he was getting too old for her acrobatics.

Soon, pretension proved a reality. Having once closed his eyes, tired by the very process of comparing and judging the trio, he was soon asleep. Perhaps the effect of the chloroform had not entirely worn off.

The bandage of the incision had been removed and Dev was happy that today Chitra would resume her physiotherapy. She arrived, wearing her starched white half-sleeved jacket, both hands in pockets, cheerful, smiling.

"How are you this morning?" she cheerfully asked her patient.

"Looking forward to the physiotherapist," replied Devendra gallantly.

"Not the physiotherapist, but the physiotherapy," corrected Chitra.

"To both the therapy and the therapist."

"So out with your hands. In fact, I will suggest that you now keep them out all the time. No longer do you have to hide them."

Taking out both his hands, he confessed, "They are my weak points, really. I am ashamed of how big and calloused they are."

Gently, she took his right hand into hers. "No need to be ashamed of such big hands which have known honest manual labour and got calloused while working on a farm, growing grain without which life would be impossible for all of us. Most of us would have starved but for the sturdy farmers of Punjab."

How sensible and intelligent she was! How gentle were her hands! How soothing was her mere touch! "Close your fist."

"Open your hands."

"Spread your fingers…like this."

"Hold my hand."

(It was a pleasure).

"Now hold it tight."

"Your grip is getting stronger!"

(I wish it were true!).

"*Shabash!* Now you *are* really getting your strength back."

"I don't think you will need physiotherapy any longer," she declared one morning after two weeks of daily exercises.

"You should not give your patients such abrupt shocks," he said it facetiously, as though he meant it to be serious. "You have to treat some patients all their lives."

"For that they have to be married to me," she replied.

"No, Miss Bhagwat…"

"*Mrs.* Bhagwat, if you don't mind."

"So you are married?"

"Yes, Mr. Kumar."

"What does Mr. Bhagwat do?"

"He is an artist, a painter."

"Where does he exhibit his paintings? I might like to pick up some of his work."

"He does not exhibit his work nor is he prepared to sell them."

"Oh, I see. You mean one of those artists who work for the sake of art. Can I see his paintings?"

"Certainly. But you will have to come to our place for coffee and *vada* one morning. Should I give you my business card, Mr. Kumar?"

She handed him a small card on which was printed:

Mrs Chitra Bhagwat

Physiotherapist

Bhindi Gali, Gamdevi, Bombay 7

"When shall you come?"

"Sooner than you expect!"

The very next morning, Devendra was up at the crack of dawn. He packed his suitcase but left it in the room. Now thanks to physiotherapy, he was fit to negotiate the long corridors of the Creak Brandy Hospital and come out in the light of the morning. He filled his lungs with the clear, cool air blowing straight from the nearby sea.

He took a taxi from the stand in front of the hospital, gave the Gamdevi address and told the driver, "I will be coming back in an hour. So keep the meter running."

"Alright, Mr. Kumar."

"So you know me?"

"Who does not know the Duper Star?"

After negotiating a few narrow lanes that were awakening to a new day, the taxi stopped before a *chawl*. When he enquired about the Bhagwats, a little urchin pointed upwards to the top of the building.

The rickety staircase on the fourth floor was where he found the signboard, "Mrs. Chitra Bhagwat, Physiotherapist." Then he rang the bell.

"*Itkya pahate kon asoo shakel*? (Who could it be this early?)" a woman's voice said in Marathi. Obviously Chitra Bhagwat's.

"*Kadachit to tuza navin mitra aala asava* (Maybe your new friend is here)," came a man's reply. "*Lavkar kar*. Duper Star *jaast vaat baghayla lavoo nakos (*Hurry up. Not nice to make stars wait.)."

Then the door opened and it was Chitra, her hair awry, in a crumpled housecoat, but as she saw him, there was the same smile on her lips.

"Welcome, Mr. Kumar. I didn't expect you this early, and so soon. Please come in."

She led him across the gallery to a room which looked like a painter's studio. There were paintings but each of them had the front turned back. There was a half-finished painting of a woman on the easel. It was not difficult to see that it was going to be a portrait of Chitra.

"This is my husband," said Chitra as the curtains parted and the artist entered in a wheelchair.

He was not much older than Chitra, and equally handsome, but he looked older because of the disorderly hair on his head that was already greying and against the morning light from the window there seemed to be a halo round his head.

"I was told you are an artist," said Devendra, "You look like a saint."

The man on the wheelchair chuckled. "Don't go by appearances. If Chitra had not warned me you were the Duper Star of the movies, I would have taken you to be a farmer from Punjab lost in the great city of Bombay."

"I *am* a farmer from the Punjab, and I am lost in this big cement concrete jungle called Bombay."

That set the tone of this friendly man-to-man conversation as Chitra retired to the kitchen via the bedroom where she had quickly arranged her hair and changed into a stiff orange organdy sari, which set off her complexion. From the kitchen, she emerged with a tray bearing three cups of coffee and plates of *vadas* and *puranpoli* (Indian snacks). There were also three quarter-plates.

She set the tray on the table between the two men, who were now discussing the merits of the Maharashtrian and the Punjabi farmers.

She handed each of them a plate with a couple of *vadas* and a *puranpoli*.

"I am really hungry. All thanks to Mrs. Bhagwat's physiotherapy," said Devendra.

"I am also an outpatient of hers," confided Anil Bhagwat, then added with a merry wink, "Isn't she like a school-mistress: do this, do that? Ordering us about all the time."

"But she put life back into my lifeless hands," said Devendra.

"And she put life into all my limbs, which were atrophied by a stroke of paralysis. She brought me home on a stretcher. Now I can move about in this wheelchair. But still I say she is too strict with her patients—too strict and too tactless. She told a fat *seth* his trouble was that he had too much fat and too much money, and prescribed that he build a room, the whole floor of which would be a hot-plate on which he would not be able to stand on his legs for a minute. That will make him perspire and reduce his weight by five pounds per day. Now how can she have patients if she behaves with them like that?"

But Devendra knew that behind all this bantering criticism was genuine admiration for his wife.

Finishing his cup of coffee, Devendra put it on the table. "I must be getting along now. Thank you very much. Both of you."

"Aren't you going to see my paintings?" asked Anil Bhagwat.

"Of course, that's why I am here. But I did not ask because you have put them all with their faces to the wall."

"To expose them is like being naked in public. That's why I am shy of displaying them to strangers."

"That means that I'm not a..." Devendra almost stammered.

"No, you are not a stranger," Anil assured him, "you are a friend. See them all then tell me which one you like best."

Each painting, as it was turned, was revealed as Chitra in her many incarnations as physiotherapist: the familiar white jacket over her sari, patient's hand in hers, tenderness and compassion in her eyes while a smile of hope hovered over her lips.

In every painting, she was shown giving exercises to her patients' limbs— now a leg, now massaging the back, now watching as a lame patient struggled with the pedals of a stationary bicycle. But the best of all was with a child whom she was teaching to walk. The painting was called."The First Step". In the painting there was such a glow of happiness on Chitra's face as she held the little patient's hand that the painter had caught with his brush.

"This is beautiful," said Devendra. "It should be called 'Mother'. It demonstrates the universal emotion of motherhood."

"Do you know what I call her? A re-educator," Anil said. "The French phrase for physiotherapy is 're-education of human limbs'."

"Well, why not say re-education of human beings? I have certainly been 're-educated' in more than one sense."

Anil gestured to Chitra, who took the painting to Anil. He took a sketch pen from his pocket and scribbled something on the back of the painting, "To my friend and fellow patient, Devendra, the greatest of the *Paanch Aadmi*."

"You have seen my *Paanch Aadmi*? It's an old movie of mine; in fact, if I am not wrong, it was my *first*."

"Yes, that's why you were still an *aadmi* (man) then," put in Chitra.

To which Anil philosophically added, "Beneath his outer skin he is still that—an *aadmi!*"

Now he handed over the painting to Devendra.

"But I thought you did not want to sell any of your paintings."

"That's right," assented the artist on the wheelchair, "I am not *selling* it. I am giving it to you as a souvenir!"

"Thank you, Mr. Bhagwat!"

Anil gave him a quizzical look.

"I am sorry. I meant, thank you, Anil."

"That's better," agreed Anil, shaking hands with Devendra.

But Chitra bid him goodbye and good luck with folded hands. The physiotherapy was over.

~

When he came back to the hospital, he saw two cars were waiting for him—his own, sent by his wife, and the other by Radha, whose driver came forward and touched his cap while opening the door.

"No, Fernandes, tell your Memsaheb I'm going home.

Then he sat in the other car and was driven away, still clutching the portrait that had been neatly wrapped in brown paper by a pair of efficient coffee-coloured hands.

~

When he hung the painting on the wall of his drawing room, his wife, with a mischievous glint in her eyes remarked: "So you have brought your physiotherapist home?"

"Darling, it will be a *home* now only because of her," said her husband."

Half a Man

Rose Cottage
Mussoorie
11 June, 1952

Darling Usha,

You must be angry with me because I did not write to you earlier. You must have assumed I have forgotten about you. Believe me (you know I tell no lies), there hasn't been a day when I didn't think about you or did not intend to write. But my mom, dad and brother conspired to keep me so preoccupied that I didn't have a moment's relief. Even before I have finished breakfast, my dear brother would insist on going horse-riding. In the beginning, I used to wear slacks, but now I have got riding habits stitched for myself and I don't seem to look all that bad. So by the time we would return from Camels Back Road, it would be past 11 and it would be time for Rummy. You know it is Dad's favourite game; he is so good at it! He has trained my brother equally well so that her darling daughter Salma shouldn't feel bad about it. Mom has also started playing with us. This goes on till lunch. After which you are ordered to have a siesta so that you remain healthy, your complexion is not affected and there are no dark circles under your eyes. And the worst is, Mom has abandoned Dad and shares my bedroom, making sure I don't chew the diamond if left alone even for a minute.

By then it is time for tea, after which it is time to go for a stroll. You know how fashion-freak Mussoorie girls are. They seem to believe that if one did not wear a new saree, salwar-suit, pyjama or a dress and didn't spend an hour on the face, nobody would take notice of them at Library Point. Oh, I forgot to mention that Dad, for once, did away with his stinginess and got a whole new wardrobe tailored for me—10 sarees including a blue chiffon with a tight golden brocade blouse, seeing me in which even you will flip for me.

Since Dad feels the place is now crowded by the riff-raffs, we don't spend too much time there, but then you can't bypass it either. Amongst this lot of the lower middle class, there are some beautiful girls as well, and some high-society boys hover around them. And the way they stare makes one wonder if their eyes had X-rays in them, undressing you mentally, making us feel as if we were skinned, headless goats hung at a butcher shop, and amongst them are some demanding the thigh portion and another breast pieces. At such moments, one suffers from giddiness and feels like tearing off one's garments, smearing the face with mud and strolling down like a hill-woman clad in rags so that those shameless, ruthless looks do not come my way.

After crossing Library Point, we land up in Heckman's Ballroom where Dad would have his fixed quota of four pegs of whisky, while my dear brother would, on the sly, quickly gulp down a glass of beer with friends on another table. Mom would, for the umpteenth time, announce that sherry was not alcohol. But for me, only a cup of coffee would be ordered. When we last came here, in the summer of 1947, I was a blue-frocked 10th standard student with no make-up, and not allowed in Heckman's Ballroom. I don't have any memories really, but Dad (who has dared to venture here after the riots) says: "There is no life or gaiety here any more!" For one, there are hardly any of his favourite Englishmen here now, and his influential Muslim friends have also migrated to Pakistan. And for those left behind, the abolition of the *zamindari* (of landed gentry) system has rendered visits to Mussoorie unaffordable. Then, the tragic events following Partition have so impacted some others that they chose not to come.

But Dad is most upset about the class of people who frequent the hill-town now: small town lawyers, doctors, officials, deputy-collectors, etc. Dad wouldn't touch them even with a barge pole! Then there are indulgent, moneyed Sindhi and Punjabi businessmen who cannot even hold themselves straight after drinking a couple of pegs. Dad labels these loud-coloured, tie and bush-shirt-sporting guys, uncouth and uncultured. He would have banished them from Mussoorie if he had his way. But the trouble is, this is the kind that's now crowding Heckmen's, along with their heavily made-up wives and daughters, dressed in the best of clothes, dancing like crazy. Some of these youngsters also invited me to dance but I declined, fearing Dad's disapproval. Not that I could dance anyway. Mom used to dance at one point but not anymore. When I asked what was wrong if I learnt dancing, he refused to entertain my query point blank, complimenting his argument with: "It was different in those days. Englishmen knew how to dance, and even the Indians belonged to the higher strata. Your mom would dance with Nawab Rampur, His Highness of Nanpada, even Sir JP, but these guys, they are just ruffians!" But when these guys stopped coming my way, he had to change his mind. Now I am allowed to learn the steps from my brother. But where is the "thrill" in dancing around with him?

So that's how I spend time, my dear. It is only around midnight when Mom starts snoring that I am alone with my thoughts. That is when, recalling the past, I think of you as well. You know what I mean, don't you? If you walk past the Department of Economics and notice someone in black trousers and a brown tweed coat (darned at the shoulder by me) do throw an inviting glance in that direction. I've been imprisoned in this golden cage but they can't put a chain around my thoughts. So it is during these lonely moments of night, before dozing off...So, okay, my dear...I am writing this letter from inside the bathroom and Mom is incessantly knocking at the door, asking me to hurry up...so will write again. Do write of the latest in Lucknow.

Give my love to Roshni, Shammi, Neeru and Naina (and how's it going, your Chand Bagh romance?).

Yours (but not exclusively yours)
Salma

~

Rose Cottage
Mussoorie
18 June, 1952

Darling Salma,

Gold bless you. Your letter reopened the door to memories of Lucknow obliterating the heavenly beauty of Mussoorie. You are complaining of loo and sweat while I want to fly back to be where you are and "he" is even if it is as hot as hell there. Don't pretend to be ignorant! As if you are not aware of my feelings for Ahmad? That was an open secret. You ask: What did I find in this uncouth, country bumpkin of a lecturer to fall in love with (and if I ask the same about that novice Nirmal who still thinks love is akin to *Vidyapati* films and Mahadevi Verma's poems!)? So, my dear, let me tell you, I love everything about Ahmad, including his wearing of a woollen coat at the peak of the summer just because I had darned it! Besides, I like his uncombed thick black hair; his deliberations on Socialism in the garb of delivering a lecture on Economics, and yes, his manner of asking: "Yes, Miss Salma Shamshad Ali Khan, you also belong to an aristocratic family, what's your opinion about the abolition of the *zamindari* system?" I like that, too. And then ...oh let it be. There would be trouble if someone else gets to read this letter.

You are wrong if you think that I am in the first flush of youth when girls seem to fall for their teachers, or rather, get infatuated by them. I don't suffer from those fleeting attacks of madness. I have liked Ahmad not since he is a Professor but from the days he was a graduate student and we were in the first year of IT College. Do you remember the day when you, Roshni and I had gone to the coffee house, where a drunken Englishman had stepped in and, seeing us girls unescorted, started acting fresh with us and we were trembling with fear? The red-faced monkey completely lost it when he lifted my veil, came so close that I could smell whisky on his breath, and said: "Come, darling, this is a night for love!" And nobody dared to interfere because he had a pistol in his holster. It was only that tall, thin, dark boy sitting silently in a corner, absorbed in a book, who quietly got up, picked up a coffee pot and crashed it on the huge Englishman's head! Do you recall the fierce fight between them? And when the Army cops took the guy away, we saw our saviour cleaning his bleeding forehead as if he was just wiping off his sweat, and telling us: "Sorry for the trouble, but now the guy dare not come anywhere near you girls." Seeing so much blood, I had literally fainted but I haven't forgotten that day! Nor has he! And whenever he looks at himself in the mirror and sees the scar on his forehead, he remembers that day…and me.

No, my dear Usha, I am not a prisoner of that schoolgirl infatuation. I have observed Ahmad in every manner: smiling, angry, even crying once. I have listened to his lessons in Economics and reciting Ghalib, Iqbal, Firaq and Majaz. He has never confessed any love for me but then I also don't agree with you "that his interest in me might just be limited to what a young professor has in any beautiful student." I am no beauty and there are several other good-looking girls in the class but he doesn't ever look at their direction. And then I am not so naive as to not distinguish between good and bad, nor have I had a veiled existence. I have met some other young men as well and if you do not mind my indulgence, Ahmad is not the first to have shown an interest in me. At the cost of your calling me shameless, I also confess that he is not my first love. But if I like him and am willing to make sacrifices there has to be a reason for that. Do you get it, my dear?

Let me also tell you that Mom, Dad and my dear brother unanimously feel that I have been so absorbed in Mussoorie's distractions that I have totally forgotten Ahmad. That's perhaps why Mom has shifted back to Dad's room. I am now at liberty to write to friends. I wrote to him last night advising him to come during the summer break. And the second is to you! It's 4 p.m. and generally we have tea together at 4.30. I had intended to write a lot more but Mom is shouting from the other room reminding me we have to join Mr. Mathur for the evening tea (boring PCS type staying in the neighbouring bungalow). I dislike the very thought but Mom and Dad take these formal social get-togethers so seriously that I will be reprimanded if I declined. So enough for the moment! Will write again...

Yours,
Salma

PS: You are fortunate to be in Lucknow and to go to the university to study, and look up "someone".

PPS: Have you watched Ram Kumar's new release *Khwab?* You must. This boy is more attractive than Dilip and Raj. Every girl in Mussoorie is mad about him.

~

Mussoorie
26 June, 1952

My dear Usha,

Lots of love!

"Ek teer mere seene pe mara ki hai hai!" (Oh gosh, the arrow has pierced my heart). River Gomti, and the reflection of Chattar Manzil in it on a moonlight night! And the Boat Club picnic with him! How romantic (and his presence in that scene at the Boat Club). And how beautifully you recapitulate the scene? I am jealous. *"Zikr us parivash ka aur phir bayaan apna..."* (Mention of him and your way of description). Did he really enquire about me? Or have you concocted all this just to tease me? Listen, I won't forgive you if you were joking in this delicate matter. I am asking you so pointedly because the letter I have got from him is so formal and matter-of-fact, devoid of any romance... "Hope you are better now and catching up at home with the classes missed in college. Should you want to understand the finer points of Communism then you must read Webb's book. But to understand the opposite point of view, it would be better if you read Brenham's *Managerial Revolution* so that you realise how ridiculous are the theories of the anti-socialists...etc., etc." Now, you only tell me, why did I have to take all the precautions to get his letters not at mine but Mrs. Mathur's address? Actually, you should also write to me only care of Mrs. Roop Kumari Mathur, Hill Lodge, Mussoorie.

And now about the Mathurs (didn't I mention them in my last letter?). This family has come to stay in the adjoining bungalow for the past couple of weeks. An interesting lot, each one a chapter culled out of a book of psychology. Mr. Mathur, PCS, is a dark, bald, pock-marked face sporting thick glasses with two decades of service and now posted as District Collector of some province. Must be around 45. His friends jokingly compare his bald pate to an egg. He is a habitual *paan* eater and uses flavoured tobacco, perhaps because he suffers from pyorrhea, and chews tobacco to counter the foul smell (one can actually smell a whiff of it when he is not chewing the betel leaves). If you want to see someone suffering from an inferiority complex, you should see him. Not only is inferiority written on his face but he also seems like a poor orphan. And because he is from PCS, he feels inferior to the ICS guys. Being bald, he feels inferior to those with hair. Being short and with a paunch, he avoids confronting tall, handsome and healthy youngsters. His father was a lawyer's *munshi,* assistant, and educated his son through scholarships; therefore, he suffers from an inferiority complex in the presence of the rich and the famous. But perhaps he is most conscious of it in the presence of his young wife.

Mrs. Mathur is elegant and beautiful, though not as majestic or ethereal like Veena and Naseem.Though she is around 28 or 30, she likes to compete with those who are much younger. She is quite pleasingly disposed towards me, but insists that I call her Roopa, "After all, we are almost of the same age," she says. And she is much interested in listening to my love escapades. Having missed romance in her own life, she seems to have become obsessively interested in listening to others' romantic experiences. The grapevine has it that she herself at one point of time contributed love stories to magazines like *Maya* and *Sarita* (she herself claims so). You might be familiar with the byline: Roop Kumari. There are rumours of her torrid romance with a young writer (a literary romance like that of Kanhaiyalal Munshi and Leelawati Munshi or one that was between Hijab Ismail and Imtiaz Ali Taj). But her parents were keen on an alliance with either an ICS, or at least a PCS. So the poor fellow abandoned his literary ambitions and competed for the PCS but lost out by just a single mark. And she was forcibly married off to Mr. Mathur.

My dear Usha, we too have gone through these exams and condemned all such competition. But have you ever contemplated lives being ruined by just a single mark? But that was six years ago. (It is a different matter that while Mr. Mathur still gets a monthly salary of Rs. 900, that writer-lover is posted as Press Attaché in the Indian Embassy in Washington and earning Rs. 1,800 a month.)

It is the same old familiar story of a young wife and an aged or much older husband. But Mr. Mathur had been married earlier as well and has a daughter from his first, illiterate and ugly wife. She proved an utter failure as the wife of a government official. According to the grapevine (i.e., the official Mussoorie scandalmonger), out of sheer nervousness, she one day gulped down the finger bowl instead of dipping her fingers in it at the Commissioner's dinner.The very same day, Mr. Mathur packed her off to her parents' (though he continues to send her a monthly stipend of Rs. 100), while sending the daughter to a convent school in Nainital. And since then, he was, for years, in search of a beautiful, educated wife, who would contribute to his social life instead of drinking away the finger bowl itself.

And finally his roving eye fell on Roop Kumari. The rest I have already narrated to you.

Now Mr. Mathur dotes on his wife and looks up to her with great reverence, is at her beck and call all the time, catering to the smallest of her needs. I have even noticed her chewing betel leaves and him providing the spittoon. Even willingly settling bills for the fabric, tailoring and jewellery, ungrudgingly. She, perhaps, has more than a hundred sarees; a countless collection of shirts and pyjamas; a matching coat for every saree; countless shoes and sandals lined up against the walls of her bedroom. Dozens of monthly and weekly periodicals and books are ordered regularly for her, but she says she has lost interest in literature and now likes to read film magazines, especially *Film India*. She can trace the lineage of every star; his date of birth and date of entry into films; each and every film he has acted in and under which banner that film was made; and which hero is "involved " with which heroine—she knows each and every detail by heart.

Only the other day, while returning from a screening of Ram Kumar's new release, *Khwab*, she asked me: "Do you know he belongs to our Lucknow and passed the Senior Cambridge exam from La Martinière? He was doing his Master's when Rustum Irani of the Royal Film Company came for a shoot and took Ram Kumar back with him to Bombay. His first film as a hero was with Vimala Rani who flipped for him; after that, whichever producer wanted to cast her had to cast Ram Kumar as well." Etc., etc...

Oh, what the hell. I have again gone off track. What I meant to suggest was while he looks after her so well, she just ignores him, to the extent that when she suffers an attack of neuralgia an hour after dinner and when even a dozen Aspirins prove ineffective, the poor husband suffers insults despite his vain attempts to massage her head with balm. In situations like this, he moves from room to room like one possessed, just like Roop's pet black cat, Juliet.The only difference being that after Roop medicates herself to sleep, Juliet snuggles at her feet under the blanket, while Mr. Mathur has to gulp down a sleeping pill in the adjoining room to induce sleep.

I take pity on their situation. But Mathur's daughter, Shammo, is even worse off. Her full name is Shyama Kumari but everyone at home addresses the 18-year-old as Shammo. Having done her Senior Cambridge from a Convent school in Nainital, she is now studying in her first year at IT College... But I must conclude now. "Food is ready," Mom is shouting from the dining room, so I will continue the Shammo saga in my next letter. You pride yourself as a "psychologist and psychoanalyst" but you wouldn't have found such specimens like the Mathurs even in your textbooks.

And do look after yourself.

With love,

And by the way, should you find "someone", do throw a glance at him, but just once, lest the "confidante" turns rival and the guy goes bonkers.

Yours,
Salma

~

Mussoorie
27 June, 1952

Dear Usha,

I did write a long letter yesterday. You'll get the two of them together. Could you please check at the University Registrar's office whether it is possible to sit for the Intermediate exam as a private student? Shammo wants to know this (she is Mr. Mathur's daughter, Shyam Kumari, who suffers from indifferent health and her father wants her to stop studying, but she wants to study at home till she recoups).

Secondly, please ask Doctor Saheb (your father) what disease causes acute stomach ache three-four times a week (alternately on both sides). Neither the X-rays show appendicitis, nor do stool examinations show the presence of any germs or dysentery. Several doctors have examined and treated her but none could pinpoint the cause.

Write urgently. In a hurry,

Yours,
Salma

PS: Don't mention anything if you come across him. What does he think of himself? It has been 10 days since I wrote to him but not a line in reply.

~

Mussoorie
3 July, 1952

Darling Usha,

Your Papa was right. Shammo's stomach ache attacks are indeed a new form of hysteria. It was a successful subconscious device to divert her father's attention towards herself from her stepmother.

How do I know, you would ask? Last Sunday, when Roop had gone to spend the day with her friend, Begum Nakshbandi (they share the same tailor and have regular weekly conferences about designs of new outfits), the whole day, Mr, Mathur played carrom with Shammo. When I went to Roop to borrow the latest issue of *Screen* (that carried a report about Ram Kumar suffering from pleurisy for many weeks, resulting in the cancellation of his under-production ventures), I found Shammo feeling better. She hadn't had an attack the whole morning. In the evening, when Mom said: "Let's go to the Mathurs," we found father and daughter having their tea, and she looked happy. Mr. Mathur asked us to join them, saying, "Let's have a cup of tea before going out for a stroll." But Roop suddenly descended and told her husband, "Lets go for a movie. Today is the last day of Ram Kumar's film *Kalank*." Mr. Mathur dutifully said, "Yes, sure. I will call and book the seats. Shammo is also feeling good and we will take her along." But Roop rudely said, "No. The doctor has advised her not to strain too much. She won't come with us. Now hurry, pick up your overcoat."

At that moment, poor Mr. Mathur looked like a schoolboy in front of his teacher. As he quietly got up to pick up his hat and overcoat, there suddenly emerged such terrible shrieks from Shammo's room that we all rushed upstairs and found her twisting and turning in her bed, crying with pain, shouting that she would die. I touched her body; it was cold with sweat on her forehead, her pupils were turned upwards and she was holding her stomach with both hands. "Salma, please call the doctor," and then, looked at his wife apologetically said: "Now forget..."

He had hardly uttered these words when she intervened and, angrily slamming her foot on the floor, said, "I anticipated this scene. Now you stay with your daughter. I'm going," then, turning towards me, she asked: "Are you coming, Salma?"

I was also keen to see the Ram Kumar film but looking at Shammo, I declined the offer, saying: "I will watch it some other time. Shammo is not feeling well at all..." but Mom intervened and said, "Don't worry, I will stay with her. You go to the movie with Roop."

So we went for the movie. I've already written to you about Ram Kumar's last starrer *Khwab* but he is brilliant in *Kalank*, essaying the role of an alcoholic poet. You know I am not particularly fond of Hindi movies (they lack the glamour and grandeur of Hollywood flicks). But whether there is anything else or not in a Ram Kumar starrer, his acting is so good that even a "super critic" like me is absolutely floored. The only weak point in the film was that squint-eyed heroine, Neelima. She can't stand up to Ram Kumar in even a single shot. I don't know how such a famous, brilliant actor agrees to work with that third-rate actress. During the film, Roop asked me, "Wouldn't a girl die of happiness if she got such a good, handsome husband like him?" I said at this point of time we should pray for Ram Kumar's health, the poor guy was suffering from a fatal disease like pleurisy. And she quietly confided, "I've prayed to God, I'll observe a day's fast and donate Rs. 10 in charity the day he regains health." And I thought, goodness gracious, she indeed is a crazy fan. How stupid of me, having strayed away from talking about Shammo. So when we returned from the movie that night we found her playing cards with Mom and Mr. Mathur. Mom told me it was about 15 minutes after we had left that Shammo began to show signs of recovery to the extent that by the time the doctor examined her, the pain had totally subsided.

That's why I said your father was 100 per cent correct. Do narrate the whole episode to him.

It's quite chilly here after the monsoon. The place is bustling with activity. At the skating rink one often runs into a group of smart youngsters from Bombay. Oh, I forgot to tell you that after having slipped several times, now I have become an expert at roller skating. It is interesting. It's two-in-one, you exercise and you dance as well. It would have been great fun if you too had been here. Alone, I am even afraid to talk to anyone. Don't know why you are stuck in Lucknow in this heat. And what to say of that dry arsine, anti-romantic chap who has written: "Enjoy Mussoorie's bourgeois cold, I am happy in Lucknow's proletariat heat." This is what I get in response to my three letters inviting him to visit Mussoorie. Fat lot of a proletariat!

I will close the narrative now before it turns into a novel and you have to needlessly dish out 15 per cent royalty to read it.

Yours,
Salma

PS: Are you mad, wanting to shift to Economics for your Master's, leaving your favourite Philosophy and Psychology? You'll realise your folly once you start attending "his" boring discourses. I can only warn you, the rest is up to you.

~

Mussoorie
11 July, 1952

Usha,

Listen to this special broadcast from Mussoorie.

Roop has recovered from neuralgia and Shammo has been cured of her stomach ache.

Mrs. Nakshbandi and Roop have ordered a dozen new designer blouses each for tailoring and I am also looking forward to some excitement from the boring Mussoorie regime. Why this swift change, you may ask? Ram Kumar is visiting here for a change of climate. And you wouldn't believe, he's neither staying at the Savoy nor the Heckman's, but with the Mathurs (to avoid crazy fans). This is an interesting story as well. One of his cousins is either a Controller or Director in a central government Supply Department in Bombay, and has an apartment in the same building where Ram Kumar lives and they share good vibes. So when the doctors advised him to shift to Mussoorie, the cousin wrote to Mr. Mathur. He was rather nervous to begin with, saying, "These film guys earning in lakhs are rather arrogant. We know nothing about this guy. Would he fit into this domestic atmosphere?" But Roop chided him: "He's convalescing. Let him come and stay with us, poor chap, wouldn't get a moment's relief in a hotel. Here we can all take care of him." Mr. Mathur instantly changed his tune: "Yes, yes. That's precisely what I meant to say. He's also from

UP…we must get him. He looks rather well-behaved on the screen."

So he's coming here next week, quickening Mussoorie's heartbeat. Sorry, have to end now. Going to Roop's to participate in a discussion on interior decoration…

Will write again when Ram Kumar is here.

Yours,
Salma

PS: If you run into your Economics professor and he asks about me, tell him I have been busy and unable to write back…I may reply next week, if time permits.

~

Mussoorie
23 July, 1952

Sorry there has been so much excitement around these past 10 days that I couldn't even respond to you earlier. The arrival of Ram Kumar has put the whole of Mussoorie, particularly the neighbourhood, on its feet. A dinner at Mr. Mathur's house one day, lunch with Mrs. Nakshbandi the next and tea at our place on the third. A picnic everyday, sometimes at the Kempty Falls, another at Bhatta Falls; yesterday at Chandal Peak and tomorrow at Toop Tibba. In short, it is excitement galore!

You asked how Ram Kumar looks in real life. Honestly, I was quiet taken aback in the first instance. He's dark complexioned (they use make-up in films), getting bald (sports a wig in films), and wears thick-glass, "intellectual" kind of frames. Normally sports trousers and a Jawahar jacket during the day. Otherwise he wears a thick tweed coat instead of formal suits (all the young boys have got themselves similar jackets). Looks more a literary type or an academic than an actor, even talks likes that. But his eyes have that fatal attraction that's visible in his face on close-ups and his voice has the strange romantic tinge that we see in his films (remember the popular belief that his voice comes not from his throat but from his heart!), the same smile that makes girls swoon with delight.

One day, Roop romantically asked him, "Ram (the first day he was Mr. Ram Kumar, the next Ramji, and now only Ram), have you been interested in acting right from your childhood?"

His reply was matter-of-fact, "No, Mrs. Mathur (she has asked him a million times to address her as Roop but he insists on calling her formally), first I wanted to be an engine driver, then a lawyer like my father. In college I got interested in Economics and was preparing for my Master's when I had to go to Bombay, otherwise by now I would have got my doctorate on Marxism."

When I heard Marxism, Economics from an actor, I was jealous (perhaps I had heard this before), so I tauntingly asked, "So, Mr. Ram Kumar (he keeps insisting that "even though I am fast losing my hair, that doesn't mean I am so senior that you address me formally. Just call me Ram!" But I insist on using the prefix), why did you abandon Marxism and join films? Was it because of a sudden desire to serve the arts?"

"Serve the arts?" he laughed, repeating my words. "Only fools do that in the film trade. To be honest, none of your college teachers and university professors is there for the sake of education. All of us actors or academics work to fill our stomachs. I became an actor when my mother couldn't afford my education after my father's death. I had applied for a clerical position in a government office and used to spend most of my time in the coffee house. One day, I met Mr. Rustam Irani there, who was in Lucknow looking for a new face. He asked me, "Would you like to be an actor?" I replied, "I don't mind if the monthly salary is at least Rs. 250 because I could get a job for Rs. 200 in Lucknow itself. So he said, 'Okay, fine.' Later, I realised he was willing to pay Rs. 500 a month... So anyway, I covered the gap in my next contract... This is the story of my becoming an actor from a human being." And he burst into laughter which sounded so hollow and unreal, kind of theatrical, as if to hide some deep-seated disappointment.

All this while, Shammo, who had been looking at him wide-eyed, asked, "Isn't an actor a human being as well?"

"No!" he said after a pause. "An actor is not a human being. Perhaps you could call him half-human...part human, part machine." Then, as if, thinking aloud, "Part human, part machine. This is the tragedy of an actor. Even though he too is made of flesh and blood with a heart and a mind, he is made to function like a machine. Press a button, he falls in love with Vimla; press a button, he is head over heels involved with a Kamala or a Neelima; press a button, he turns into a wastrel prince, a romantic poet, a Devdas; now laughing, now crying and singing, and then he is expected to bring an element of realism to both the wastrel and the pious, look natural while laughing or crying, drink real alcohol, consume real poison. And after all this, he's expected to be a celibate, a saint, after performing intense love scenes inside a studio.

Only a superman who exists above natural emotions or a half-human, that is, an actor, can do these emotional acrobatics...the unfortunate machine that transforms acting into real, until acting becomes a part of his personality."

Very interesting, more interesting than the dialogues he mouths on screen. One just wants to sit there and listen. We return home past midnight when these sessions conclude in Roop's living room and are back after breakfast the very next day to pick up threads from the previous night.

Oh, I forgot to mention. Shammo hasn't had another attack and is now fully cured of aches and pains. Can you guess who treated her...Ram Kumar. He's an amateur doctor as well. A strong advocate of homeopathy, he says it was homeopathy that cured him of pleurisy and not allopathic injections. And had he been injected some more, he would have become just like a sieve. Now, he not only reads homeopathy books but also dispenses medicines, advocates the system and carries a black leather bag full of little bottles. We often tease him about this. Someone saying if there is no other sweet dish, let's gulp down sweet little homeopathy balls, while others make fun of his diagnosis and prescription, that were actually nothing but sugarballs. But there is no doubt he cured Roop of her neuralgia. Shammo also does not get her attacks of pain. But you could also say it was his presence that made all the difference.

Even Mr. Mathur is now an admirer of his because Ram Kumar has a cure for his status consciousness as well. They play chess for hours on end. He boasts of being amongst the best 10-12 chess players in Bombay but Mr. Mathur is one up on him. He is the master of the game, when he moves his pieces, it seems as if a General is placing his forces in a battlefield, totally forgetting about his bald head, smallpox marks, pyorrhea stench, and age. That's perhaps why he tried to engage the least interested Roop in the game.

So this is my life pattern these days. The distant Savoy hotel clock gongs midnight and one is off to picnic tomorrow. So it's goodbye for now.

Yours,
Salma

~

Mussoorie
8 August, 1952

Dear Usha,

Sorry for the inordinate delay in responding. I've been upset and there's no one around to share it with. Had you been here I would have poured my heart out to you and felt somewhat relieved. So now I have decided to do so through this letter. I know Dad brought me here to forget Ahmad, but I wasn't aware of the other conspiracies behind the move as well.

Yesterday we got a guest from Pakistan who Dad patronisingly addresses as "my boy"—Chaudhry Hanifullah. Must be around 50, can write his name in English and does not hold the newspaper upside down. Earlier. he had been involved in the leather trade in Kanpur when, he proudly says, his firm exported belts to England and America worth millions (and in the process added quite a bit to his girth). He doesn't react to a joke and gulps down a taunt like a soft drink. When the division of the country was announced in June '47, he quietly disposed of his business and property and transferred the money to Pakistan. Now he works as a government contractor in Lahore. Dad knew his father well, so he accepted his invitation and travelled not only to India but to Mussoorie. He is always worried about his money and life (because of the Income Tax liabilities due at the time of migration that could lead to arrest, should the concerned authorities here find out about his presence in India).

So he looks at every Hindu or Sikh with suspicion, lest one of them pushes a knife into him. He treats Muslims like us, like goats that could be slaughtered any time. Stupid fool! His activities could have been fun, but he has been invited here as a "Prospective Groom". Dad wants to marry me off to him (hoping that with Hanif Saheb's influence, he would also be able to acquire business and property in Pakistan) and I feel exasperated at Mr Hanifullah's general attitude towards us, as if he was doing us a favour. I don't know what to do. Sometimes I think of running away from home, taking up a job somewhere and escaping from this butcher. But these things look good in stories and novels, in reality it is not so. Where should I go, live, find a job? Thousands of graduate women like me are loitering around in search of a job. You can't live on a schoolteacher's take-home salary and annoy and defy your parents for his sake? Can you?

Who else do I have in the world? Ahmad hardly has time for someone's feelings other than Economics and Marxism. Besides, I don't want to stoop so low as to force myself on him. So, the days are going by in this confusion and to top it all, Hanif Saheb keeps haranguing about belts and shoes. And if that is not enough, I have to listen to Mom and my dear brother trying to convince me that all the rich, educated, influential young Muslims had already migrated to Pakistan and there were hardly any left in India, and Dad indirectly keeps counting Hanif's virtues—the empire, the millions worth of property, a leather factory, a cinema theatre, government contracts and what not; a beautiful summer cottage in Murree, three cars and the works... But that doesn't interest me, you know. Not the prospects.

Haven't met Ram Kumar for the past two days, nor been to the Mathurs, who must be wondering what's wrong with me. But then, one has to play up to Hanif to appease the parents.

I now feel light-hearted having shared my feelings with you. Let's hope there would be a way out of this rigmarole. Do write soon. Your letters are like a soothing balm.

Yours,
Salma

~

Mussoorie
18 August, 1952

Dear Usha,

The good news first. Hanif Saheb is packing up his bag and baggage for Pakistan, upsetting my family because he has refused to marry me. I am happy, bursting at the seams. This is an interesting story, rather, a screenplay with Ram Kumar as the hero.

As I was approaching the Mathur house on the third day, I found Ram Kumar in our house. Brother dear had taken Hanif to the post office (he probably had to shoot off an urgent telegram and rather than relying on servants, preferred to attend to it himself) while Mom and Dad were having an afternoon siesta. As I was playing with the radio knobs, the door opened and someone was shouting, "Hi, Salma." Ram Kumar walked in, pushing the door open, and continued, "I hope all is well. You look sick. Should I give you a dose of 'sugar' or is it some sort of an emotional fever? I believe a Pakistani Don Juan is here." He said all this in such a soft, concerned voice with so much sympathy, but in a light banter, that I literally burst into tears.

"Now this is not done, Salma. You're behaving like a kid. What's the problem?"

Unable to hold back I told him the reason for Hanif's visit. He contemplated for a while, then said, "So that's it. Now what should we do about it?"

A daring thought crossed my mind, and I just spelt it out, "You can solve this problem, Ram Saheb."

"Me! How can I?" He replied somewhat hesitantly.

"If you start taking an interest in me for some days," I mustered up the courage to suggest, "a shocked Hanif would simply run away."

"Oh, I see." His eyes brightened up like that of a child who suddenly finds a favourite toy. "Well, why only pretend? It's simple, not difficult at all to be interested in you, actually."

Saying this, he burst into laughter as if he had cracked a joke! Otherwise, why would someone with whom half the beautiful young Indian girls are in love take an interest in me? But he said, "Okay, now you wait. I'll parcel this guy out of here."

Apprehending my hesitation, even before I could utter a word, he said, "The scene starts right away."

Just then, we heard the lawn gate open and shut and we heard their steps. Ram Kumar got up, moved and, occupying the armrest of my chair, started to lovingly caress my hair.

I nearly fainted with apprehension when they walked into the room. Ram Kumar also quickly moved away as if a thief had been caught in the act (he was simply performing, I realised later), swiftly moved towards my brother and shook his hand, saying, "Hi, Salim, how're you? Long time no see!" and turning towards Hanif, "Won't you introduce me to your friend?"

Bhaijaan somehow held back his anger and introduced the two: "This is our friend, Mr. Hanifullah from Pakistan, and this is Mr. Ram Kumar. The famous actor you must have seen on the screen."

"Oh, an actor!" The manner of speech hardly hid the hatred. "No, I haven't. I've my own theatre, but I don't watch movies. Neither do I have time nor any real interest."

"That's right, what's there in cinema? The shoemaking industry is far more interesting," replied Ram Kumar. Then quickly turning towards my brother, asked, "Coming to the skating rink?"

With disapproval writ large on his face, he replied, "No, you go ahead, I have matters to discuss with Hanif Saheb."

"Alright, bye, Hanif Saheb," and leaving those two stumped, he took my hand, "Okay, Salma, let's go."

Once outside in the lawns, he freed my hand, saying: "Rest assured. He's not going to marry you now. But as my fee, you have to accompany me to the skating rink."

We spent the next two hours at the skating rink, all eyes on us, young girls jealous of me. Around 5 p.m., Hanif and Salim came there but turned back instantly. Before they could do that, Ram Kumar, who moved like a professional, caught them at the exit door, "Where is the twosome heading, come on?"

"Thanks, but we are going to Heckman's," said Hanif, before the two walked away.

A while later, Ram Kumar said, "Let's go to Heckman's and dance. I hope you know dancing?"

"Well, a little bit, but I didn't know you are good at it."

"I learnt it at some point of time but gave it up because I didn't really enjoy it. But will have to have a go at it today...duty after all."

Mom and Dad hadn't arrived when we reached there while Hanif and Salim sat drinking at a corner table. I overheard him saying, "One can't drink openly in Pakistan because of the *shariyat* (Muslim personal law), but here, no problem."

The band played "The Blue Danube" waltz as we moved to the dance floor. The lights dimmed, the music leading us to a far corner as we tapped our feet. But despite the dim lights, he neither made an attempt at kissing nor drawing me closer to his body, seemingly having set limits and being conscious of that fact. Yes, but whenever we neared Hanif and Salim's table, he pretended to move his face closer. I could feel his warm breath, making it difficult for me to distinguish between the real and the make-believe.

When the music stopped and the lights came on, the twosome had disappeared though Mom and Dad were on another table.

He greeted Dad warmly and exchanged greetings with Mom, saying, "Your daughter will be an accomplished dancer with a little more practice." You know Dad, being very conscious of courtesy and social ethics, didn't show his anger and kept the semblance of a dialogue going with him, but when the clock struck 7 p.m., he said, "Let's get back home, Salma. Hanif Saheb must be waiting for us."

But before Dad could go on, Ram Kumar intervened, "But Kunwar Saheb, Salma is dining at the Mathurs' tonight. Actually, it is my birthday today, so she has to come. We wanted to invite you as well but since you had guests...!"

Dad reluctantly granted permission.

On the way back during the rickshaw ride, I asked, "I didn't know it was your birthday today, otherwise I would have brought you a gift."

"Birthday!" He feigned forgetfulness. "Birthday, yes! What's there about an actor's birthday," he said, heaving a sigh that was lost in the hollow of his laughter, "an actor is born everyday...and dies the same day."

Mathur's living room bore a deserted look, with him alone playing with the chess pieces when we walked in. He looked up, lines of worry visible on his forehead, and said, "Give her a dose, Ram. Roop has had another attack of neuralgia."

By the time he opened the black box, we heard cries from another room. Both me and Mr. Mathur rushed in the direction to find Shammo on the bed crying with pain. Then taking charge of his daughter, Ram asked me to get her medicine. Having administered a dose with almost instant relief, and without responding to her "thank you", he stepped into the adjoining room to attend to Roop, who too showed signs of recovery in no time, saying, "Listen, Mrs. Mathur you should be up in about half an hour. It's my birthday today, so we are all going to the movies after dinner."

When he stepped out, I asked him about the miracle medicine he had administered to both. He said: "Ignatia is beneficial in all forms of hysteria attacks."

Believe me, not only did both of them recover in half an hour but also returned to the dining table and came for the movie too. When he invited me also, I told him, "You are ensuring that I am thrown out of the house." His reply simply floored me: "Maybe that's the solution to your troubles. You're at your doorstep but don't want to go in, nor do you have the courage to step out. In such a situation, the only way out for you is to be thrown out, otherwise you will remain suspended at the doorstep itself—one foot inside, the other outside."

When I stepped into the house, I found Dad waiting for me near the fireplace. Angry, he had hardly said: "You've come now!" when Hanif Saheb stepped inside in a dressing gown, then staring at me quietly, moved closer to Dad, saying, "In Pakistan, people shave the heads of their shameless daughters."

It enraged me! But I decided to remain silent, knowing very well that Dad wouldn't reprimand me in front of a guest. So I quickly slipped into my room, shut the lights, closed the door, and jumped into bed.

From the next day, I decided to be on the offensive because the only way to get rid of Hanif Saheb was to be with Ram Kumar. We would go out for a stroll in the evening, all eyes on us at Library Point, girls staring jealously, boys with changed looks as if feeling sorry for not taking the initiative. We were seen together everywhere—the skating rink, Heckman's ballroom, and the theatre. One newspaper even reported our engagement, and the new issue of *Screen* had our picture splashed on the front page (you might have noticed this too). As a result, Hanif Saheb has not only stopped talking to me, he has also started packing his bag and baggage.

Both Mom and Dad are angry, and Salim Bhai makes no bones about it. I know I am in for trouble once Hanif Saheb leaves but the consolation is, he's going. I'm ready for the consequences.

Yours,
Salma

PS: Please, keep all this to yourself only.

~

Mussoorie
29 August, 1952

Darling Usha,

Thanks for both your letters. You need not be partial towards your professor because you have started studying Economics. I'm not going to respond to his mail where he writes, "I believe that joker Ram Kumar is in Mussoorie these days and all the rich girls are moving around him like bees." Ask him to look at his face in the mirror before casting aspersions on Ram Kumar! But if he thinks it was a joke, tell him I don't like it.

It seems you also look at film actors with suspicion. How did you come to think he too is shallow and cheap?

You'll also flip for him if you listen to him. He's more in tune with what's happening around the world than many professors (especially professors of Economics). While on a walk the other day, I asked him, "You've been here for a while but haven't told us anything about the film world."

He replied: "Don't push me back into a quagmire from which I am seeking escape," then pondering awhile, continued, "I wonder, what aspect of the film world I should reveal—talk about those handsome loveless stars; the heroines who charge in lakhs for every picture, slog day and night so that their kith and kin squander away all that wealth in alcohol, gambling, racing, on prostitutes; sport shark skin suits and drive away in Buicks or Packards; or those who have millions in their bank accounts, yet don't get even a week off for years together; those who palm off plots of American movies as their own stories and sell them for huge sums, or those who just about earn in the hundreds for their original stories, dialogue and songs but find others' names in the title credits; those junior artists who feature in crowd scenes for paltry sums, hoping their fortunes will turn someday and they get a chance to replace the likes of Ashok Kumar, Motilal or Raj Kapoor; those whose studio boys and light boys risk their lives monkeying up the ropes to set up heavy lights on wooden planks, earning only a rupee or two a day; or those girls from decent homes whose characters are worse than prostitutes in brothels, or of those whores who are more pious than many; the fools who consider themselves geniuses; the geniuses who others think are fools? The film world is as multi-coloured as the rest of the world, Salma."

How can someone with such a philosophic outlook be called cheap?

I felt both angry and amused at the same time at what you wrote: "He's an actor, keep a safe distance!" Angry because you too, like others, think film stars are ruffians who sexually exploit young innocent girls, and equate Ram Kumar with them. And amused because your fears are wrong. We have been by ourselves for the past many weeks during the day and at night we have walked down long distances and danced together, but not once has he taken any liberties with me, he has behaved like a true gentleman to the extent of being boring. He's informal, even flirtatious; jokes with me when others are around, but when both of us are alone, he keeps a safe distance.

The point I am making, Usha, is that while you have seen the actor Ram Kumar on the screen, I have had the occasion of watching "the man, Ram Kumar", in person. I won't even hide the fact that I have begun to like him, and, perhaps he is attracted toward me as well. You know what he said the other day? He said, "You're the first girl in my life with whom I can freely talk like a friend."

I am beginning to feel that despite all the fame and fortune, the thing he has missed in life is love. It sounds strange that one who has thousands of young girls head over heels in love with him, or who has made love to all the beautiful heroines on screen, should feel the absence of love in his personal life. But then that seems to be the truth! The fact is, Salma, he confessed to me one day, "Love cannot last without trust and understanding, and how many of us really understand ourselves to measure up to others?" Then, looking the other way, he asked: "Have you ever loved someone, Salma? No, not ordinary infatuation that one feels in the breezy atmosphere of Mussoorie or Nainital momentarily, but real love that fills up life with colours, music and happiness, and which also familiarises one with pain and angst. This love thing is also an ailment.

I don't know how and why I felt, I should reveal to him what I had been keeping to myself all this while, because it somehow seemed to me that he could gauge my feelings and my apprehensions better than me. I told him the truth about Ahmad—how we met, began to get closer, our mutual agreements and disagreements on issues. I also told him about his intellectual capabilities, his self respect etc. because "my father is an influential man, and he, merely a lecturer, earning a modest Rs. 250 a month, he neither talks about marriage nor has he ever admitted his love towards me. So how long can one love anyone or wait indefinitely?"

He smilingly replied, "Love doesn't accept any logic, and wait...one can wait all his life if there is something worth waiting for." Then looking straight into my eyes: "Yes, Salma wait all life." And then hiding his emotions and assuming a lighthearted tone, he asked, "But who's this lucky penniless professor?"

"You wouldn't know him. His name is Ahmad!"

"Ahmad? You don't mean Ahmad Husain, do you?"

"Yes, the same guy. Do you know him?"

"Yes, I was also a student of Economics."

He then swiftly changed the subject and began psychoanalysing the Mathur family on the way back home.

So, my dear Usha I am now at the crossroads of my love life. You're the only confidante I can seek advice from. Please don't mention all this to anyone, but do write!

Salma

Mussoorie
14 September, 1952

Usha,

I often think: Is life a tragedy or a comedy? Or a tragi-comedy or comi-tragedy? Or a meaningless puppet show in which God is pulling the strings, making humans sit or stand, laugh or cry (or as we read in Marxist-Economic books, our social, political and personal lives, even our feelings and emotions are choreographed by Him)?

The twists and turns I have experienced in the recent past bring both tears and laughter at once to my eyes.

A few days after I had narrated my conversations with Ram Kumar to you, I had gone to the Mathur household one morning. I found both Roop and Shammo down with severe attacks of neuralgia and stomach ache. The moment Mr. Mathur saw me, he enquired, "Salma dear, do you know what medicines Ram used to administer to them? Just take them out of the black box that he has left behind in a hurry."

"Left behind? Has he left?"

"Yes, he got a telegram at 1 a.m. at night wanting him back in Bombay immediately. There is the *muhurat* (auspicious first shot) of his new film, *Adhure Sapne,* so he left very early in the morning. But please hurry and take out the medicines."

I was stunned when I opened the medicine box: all those small bottles were missing, except one labeled "Ignatia" with an inscription in Ram's handwriting: "Effective in all hysteria attacks, if taken intoning 'Ram'! Sure to produce desired result."

I repeated the inscription to Shammo with the medicine. Hearing that, despite the pain, she burst into laughter, then pulling out a notebook from under her pillow, said, "He had a great sense of humour. Just see what he had noted in my autograph book? He had written in his peculiar handwriting: 'Laughter is very effective in case of stomach aches. The only condition is that the patient must develop the ability to laugh at himself.'"

"The devil of him," said Roop, taking a dose, "he has autographed an old cinema ticket under which he wrote 'Half the head in pain is better than full; it at least leaves space to think, provided one has the capacity to think instead of feeling the pain.' And burst out laughing."

I felt his medicine had worked in his absence as well. Then I enquired from Mr. Mathur whether he had left any letter, any message for me.

"No, nothing!" Then, remembering something, he said, "He has left your autograph book. Here it is!"

I quickly shuffled the pages: "The truth of life is far more interesting than the shadows on cinema screens... A man is better than half-a-man."

'Half-a-man?' A smile crossed my lips recalling Ram's definition of a good actor even though I had tears in my eyes. 'But what exactly did he mean by a man?' The thought had still been reverberating in my mind when I heard someone calling me softly from behind my back. I turned around to find a smiling Ahmad (in the same tweed coat that I had darned).

"Ahmad!" I cried out aloud. "How and when did you come here?"

"Right now, straightaway. How're you feeling now?"

"What's wrong with me?"

"But he has written that a renowned homeopath has diagnosed that you are suffering from a suspected heart ailment."

"What nonsense? Which fool has told you this?"

"That idiot Ram Kumar. Where's he?"

Ram Kumar! My mind tried to resolve the puzzle: "What have you got to do with him, and how do you know him?"

He settled himself on a chair: "Who else would know that rascal better? We've studied together, both in school and college, for 15 years, including the six years we shared the hostel room. It was because of him that I studied Economics for my Master's because we were going to do our research together and you ask me how I know him. For you, he might be a great actor but I still consider him to be a fool. Where the hell is he anyway?"

"But he has left," Mr. Mathur butted in.

"Now look what the fool has done; summoned me from such a distance and disappeared himself."

"What do you propose to do now?" I enquired on way to my house.

"What do I propose to do?" He repeated, then suddenly stopped, and without paying any attention to the passersby, looked straight into my eyes, and said, "I'm going to tell your Dad right now that I want to marry you. We will get married tomorrow, and..."

"And...?" Totally stumped at the gumption, I even forgot to express my anger at his unilateral decision!

"And the day after, we'll take off to Bombay where I will conduct my research on the plight of the mill workers. Ram has also written to say we could stay with him."

"No, I won't go to Bombay,"

"That means you agree to all else. How does it matter to me whether it's Bombay, Calcutta, or even Kanpur for that matter? But we do have a friend in Bombay."

"I don't like your friend."

"You mean Ram? One has to have a little intelligence to appreciate him," he said, laughing away, and held my hand as we talked. I didn't know whether to hit him, scratch him, or embrace him and cry?

Then, believe it or not, the manner in which he spoke, Dad instantly okayed it but sought at least 10 days' time. So we're getting married here in Mussoorie next week, on September 24, and your presence is a must. I would be very angry otherwise, do you understand? So treat this letter as a telegram and rush.

Rest when we meet.

Yours, flabbergasted but happy,

Salma

~

Mussoorie
23 September, 1952

Dear Usha,

We went for a walk last night. The library, as usual, was crowded with carefree young men and colourful butterfly girls. But somehow the boys' smiles carried a worried look while the butterflies looked pale. But Ahmad's presence was the saving grace. We went to Heckman's and the skating rink for a while, but both places wore a deserted look. The crowd had been thin. The few tired faces at the bar seemed to be sipping poison, not whisky; the band played such a melancholy tune that death alone can dance, not humans. On our return, we could see the lights wrapped in fog. With the rickshaw-pullers on a two-day strike, people walked down the Mall briskly hiding heads in coat collars.

"It seems like the whole town is sleeping, wrapped up in a blanket."

"Is it asleep, or dying?" questioned Ahmad.

Salim Bhai butted in, "October is round the corner, and the season is almost over." Then, pondering, he said, "Yes the season is over, perhaps, forever..."

Your letter was waiting when we reached home. Thanks for the greetings! Sorry you won't be here tomorrow, and your health is a matter of great concern to me. Your father is himself a doctor, so get yourself thoroughly examined and should the X-ray indicate an enlarged appendix, do intimate and I shall come over to be with you.

Please don't mind this hurried note. You can imagine the activity at home, and the mood I am in.

Yours,
Salma

PS: Do write, should it just be a routine stomach ache and not an enlarged appendix, I would send you a dose of Ignatia. Think of Ram and gulp it down. It will surely work.

PPS: Stupid of you to have first shifted from Psychology and Philosophy to Economics, and now switching over to English Literature.

(Translated from the Urdu by Suresh Kohli & Dr. Zoya Zaidi)

A Conversation With Abbas

This interview with Khwaja Ahmad Abbas was conducted on 15 December, 1970, in the *Indian & Foreign Review.* Suresh Kohli discusses films and changing times in Indian cinema.

SK: Mr. Abbas, could you tell us of your experiences in the star-studded and star-dominated film industry? You also, at one time, worked with stars. Why did you suddenly switch over to new faces in your films?

KAA: Well, once upon a time I used to take quite important and very good and capable artistes who are known as stars today. At that time, the star system had not become as "impossible" as it is today, nor was it so expensive. But still, there was the star system, and I compromised with it to the extent that I took some of these stars. Not because they were stars, but because I thought they were competent and capable artistes. There was a period when I made *Anhonee* (with Raj Kapoor and Nargis), *Rahi* (Dev Anand and Nalini Jayawant) and then I made the songless *Munna,* which did not have any stars, but afterwards I made one film in which, as certain people said, I took stars with a vengeance. It was *Char Dil*

Char Rahein. It was a peculiar kind of story, with three different sets of characters representing three different classes. And, therefore, I needed Raj Kapoor and Meena Kumari in one episode, I needed Shammi Kapoor and Kumkum in another, and Ajit, Nimmi and Jairaj in the third episode.

But after that, as the star system developed and became more irresponsible, I decided not to take stars. If I had a quarrel, it was with the system itself. Each star had 15 to 20, sometimes even 30, films, and was expecting and demanding a great deal of money which I could not afford. Moreover, I could not afford to take a person who was not able to concentrate exclusively on my story and my script. And, therefore, I shifted to a no-star basis in my films.

I wanted to make an experimental film called *Shehar Aur Sapna*, to shoot on actual locations, in the city streets where the well-known faces of the stars would create serious problems. So I decided to take new artistes, and at that time, the Film Institute had not been founded and, therefore, I looked around to find people from the stage or from schools or from my acquaintances who could be shaped into artistes, those who would have the calibre to make good artistes. So I chose two young people in *Shehar Aur Sapna*. One was at that time an assistant to my good friend Hrishikesh Mukherjee, a young man called Dileep Raj. I saw in him great potential for the role I wanted to give him. The other was a young girl called Surekha whom I had seen in a school drama where I was judging the performances. So I took them up and, instead of sending them to an institute, which was non-existent at the time, I trained them myself for several months before they faced the camera.

Since then, I have found this experience very rewarding because almost all the artistes I have taken up, have proved their calibre, to the extent that Dileep Raj and Surekha were voted the two best young artistes at the Karlovy Vary Film Festival, then Jalal Agha received Special Commendation in the National Awards for his role in *Bambai Raat Ki Bahon Mein,* and now Amitabh Bachchan has got Special Commendation in the National Awards for his work in *Saat Hindustani.*

SK: What do you think of the recent phenomenon of "low-budget" experimental films in India? In a way, this is not new because some of our talented producers and directors, like yourself, have been practising the idea.

KAA: I agree with you that it is not entirely a new phenomenon, but it is now receiving new incentives. I and some others who made experimental and low-budget films had to struggle against almost insurmountable financial difficulties. For instance, compare the two different circumstances: it took me three years to make *Shehar Aur Sapna*, but it took my friend, Mrinal Sen, or my other friend, Basu Chatterji, just one month to shoot their films, *Bhuvan Shome* and *Sara Akash*. The new favourable circumstance was the creation of the Film Finance Corporation, not only the creation, but also the new policy adopted by the Corporation. I think it is very good that the Corporation is not financing the usual commercial formula films but backing new ventures by enterprising young directors with fresh ideas who would not otherwise easily find finances to make their films. This way it helps intelligent artistes to experiment with narrative styles and new techniques which, for instance, have been used in *Bhuvan Shome*, *Sara Akash* and, more recently, in *Uski Roti*.

SK: Have you seen any recent Indian documentaries? If so, what are your impressions? I personally think there have been a good number of excellent short films in the recent past.

KAA: I think the very recent documentaries are not as important and impressive as the documentaries which were produced, say, two or three years ago. For instance, documentaries like *I Am Twenty*, which was produced at the time of the 20th anniversary of Independence, or *Framework of Fortune*, a documentary like *India '67* by Sukhdev and, more recently, his documentary about the Nehru Museum which, I think, is called *Thoughts on a Museum*. Amongst the very recent ones, I have been greatly impressed by B.D. Garga's film on Amrita Shergill which is a tribute to a wonderful personality and a great artist. So I find in the world of documentaries, there is a remarkable new wave of fresh ideas and fresh talent.

But unfortunately, it is not reflected as much as it should on the screens, because the opportunities for independent documentary-makers are not adequate enough. The screening time is monopolised by the Films Division, but this organisation has a very limited budget to acquire outside productions. If this movement has to grow, then there should be a greater allocation of budget for the Films Division to acquire at least 12 short films in a year from independent producers who are making documentaries on their own, according to their own ideas.

SK: What do you think of the growing stress on sex and nudity in international cinema? Do you think it is a healthy attitude to be obsessed with these things? Aren't we forgetting the basic idea of filmmaking?

KAA: I am not at all happy with this preoccupation with sex, and along with sex, themes of violence. I think there is an economic and social reason for it, as there is for the preponderance of songs in Indian films. Western cinema is competing with television and, therefore, it has all the time to think of gimmicks that are not possible for TV. First, there was a rash of colour movies but it was balanced by TV also coming into the colour field. Then Cinemascope, Vistavision, and all the different big-screen techniques were used to attract audiences and to dazzle them with the technical brilliance not possible on the small TV screen. Now even those technical gimmicks have become routine and again the audiences were falling, so they had to adopt some other means to attract the audiences.

I think, consciously or subconsciously, that is the reason these new erotic films, what I would call erotic cinema, has come into being. I find that sex and violence in many of the Western films have become a cliché, just like songs in Indian films. Some of the very serious and artistic films have been spoiled, in my opinion, by the intrusion of these obviously forced-in scenes of sex and violence, just as many of the good Indian films are spoiled by the intrusion of songs and dances.

SK: As a serious filmmaker, how do you react to the idea of the setting up of a Film Council? Do you think it would be for the betterment of Indian cinema?

KAA: I believe that Indian cinema—which many call the film industry but I don't because I don't think it is an industry but an art and prefer to call it Indian cinema—is in a bad way. Financially, many of the big budget films are flopping, crores of rupees are going down the drain, and score of films are lying unfinished, which means millions of rupees are locked up in these films and are unproductive. There is a lack of cinema theatres, so films are lying unreleased for months and sometimes, years. Star prices have reached astronomical proportions, and the producers who are themselves responsible for raising the prices of the stars are now aghast at what the stars are demanding and expecting. And from all these points of view, there is need for a more rational organisation. Personally, I would have liked the industry to be fully nationalised. That is, there should be a complete social control over the choice of material and also control over the people who would use these materials.

SK: But, Mr. Abbas, if the Indian film industry, or, as you say, Indian cinema, was nationalised, don't you think the power would be completely in the hands of bureaucrats, and things would become difficult for filmmakers as well as creative artistes?

KAA: I am aware of these dangers—in demanding nationalisation of cinema, I am taking what you might call a calculated risk. But I think it is a risk worth taking—in other words, the alternative of going on with the present trends is infinitely worse and more dangerous than any muddle that the bureaucracy can create. You see, bureaucrats cannot make films—films will continue to be made by filmmakers. At worst, the bureaucracy can be muddle-headed, inefficient, interfering, unimaginative—and probably in the beginning, it will be all this, and many dull and uninspiring films will be made—but eventually, the law of Supply and Demand will operate. The public will reject the dull and uninteresting films (as it did in the Stalinist days in the USSR); no government can afford to indefinitely lose money on producing dull films. Then the filmmakers will get back their artistic and creative independence within the framework of social purposes and aesthetic standards, in the interests of the people.

What I am aiming at is the elimination of the commercial interests competing with each other to purvey vulgarity, titillating suggestiveness (because of censorship) which is worse than downright pornography, and spreading the artificial, escapist and un-Indian culture through films which appeal to the lowest common denominator of what is called "popular taste". In nationalised cinema, there will be competition between films that are socially useful and interesting and artistic. Of course, there will be different genres of films—comedies, musical romances, social purpose films, experimental films and art films.

But that is all in the future. At present, mine is the lone voice for nationalisation.

And therefore, I think the Film Council is an excellent idea. It is an attempt to use the best brains in cinema, and the best brains outside cinema, to sit down around a table and to plan and organise the working of Indian cinema. So I think the sooner the Film Council comes into being, the better it would be for all of us. But I would also make a reservation—it will, to a great extent, depend on the composition of the Film Council. If it is just a collection of people representing the art of the cinema, not the potentialities of cinema for doing good to the society as a whole, but sectional interest like distributors, producers and exhibitors, film critics and bureaucrats, then it will become a kind of arena where one interest will be clashing with other interests.

SK: You also belonged to—and perhaps still do—to the Progressive Writers' Movement. The movement seems to be slowing down. Could you comment on this, please?

KAA: I agree that the organisational aspect of the movement has suffered an eclipse, which I think is natural. In the beginning phase, the movement required a definitive organisation of writers to give a creative push to the progressive trends in literature. But now, I think, the movement has become a part of Indian literature itself. Therefore, today I do not think there is the same urgent need of having a regular organisation. I do not think we can judge the quality of progressive literature only by the organisational functioning of one association like the Progressive Writers' Association that may or may not be active, but the idea with which it began, with which it became a driving force during the last 30 years or so, created a certain consciousness not in writers alone but also among readers. That consciousness has become an enduring part of Indian intellectual life. And, therefore, I do not agree when people say that the Progressive Writers' Movement has become stagnant or redundant in India.

SK: What do you think is the image of Indian cinema abroad? Perhaps you could tell us something from what your experiences have been?

KAA: Well, "abroad" is a very general term. In the Middle East and the Far East and in England, where a substantial number of Indian immigrants have settled, like different countries of Africa, Singapore, Malaysia and Hong Kong, and also some of the other artistically backward countries—more backward than even India, the glossier commercial Indian films are very popular. They have also become the victims of our star system.

But apart from this, there are other countries of Europe and America where Indian cinema is virtually unknown, except for the works of Satyajit Ray which have had a certain measure of success in what I would call the art theatre circuit. His works are known to all the critics and connoisseurs of world cinema, and also are known and appreciated by a small minority of art theatre audiences, both in Europe and America.

But beyond that, I think it is unfortunate that the works of other artistic and socially conscious and important directors are unknown in the Western world. I think there is a need to stimulate interest in this, the artistically more important Indian cinema.

I think the attitude of some of the Western critics that Indian cinema began and ended with Satyajit Ray is unfair to Satyajit Ray himself, because I believe he is a very important and intelligent film director. I would like to say something more about him. I think he is an important cultural and artistic phenomenon of our times, but I do not regard that phenomenon to have grown in isolation. I regard it as a part of the Bengali cultural renaissance which was represented by Tagore, Sarat Chandra Chatterjee, Bankim Chandra Chatterjee, Qazi Nazrul Islam; by the great painters of Bengal like

Jamini Roy and by the great film makers of Bengal like Devaki Bose, P.C. Barua, Nitin Bose and Bimal Roy. And then there was also a tradition of artistic and purposeful films in India like the early works of Shantaram. So, out of all this renaissance has emerged the great personality of Satyajit Ray. He started where others left. He is carrying on the tradition. Of course, he has carried it further and I believe after Satyajit Ray there are very significant directors who are carrying this tradition further. I think their works should also be known outside and there should be an overall picture of Indian cinema available. And, through cinema, of Indian life itself.

SK: Could you perhaps name some of these other competent and socially conscious directors whose works should be better known abroad?

KAA: Well, you are setting a trap for me, aren't you? Every critic, every filmmaker, will have his own list of preferences and each list would provoke a controversy. In this list I would put most of the pictures of Tapan Sinha, especially *Atithi* which, I think, is a little masterpiece; all the works of Mrinal Sen, especially *Bhuvan Shome*; some of the films of Ritwik Ghatak. From Bombay, I would choose Raj Kapoor's *Awara, Shree 420* and *Sangam,* and his latest magnum opus, *Mera Naam Joker*; some of the works of Hrishikesh Mukherjee like *Musafir, Anari, Anuradha, Anupama* and even *Satyakam*. K. Asif's *Mughal-e-Azam* which is a monumental movie in the historical genre; Sunil Dutt's *Yaadein* and perhaps *Reshma Aur Shera;* Kamal Amrohi's *Daira;* Basu Bhattacharya's

Teesri Kasam; some of the films of Asit Sen like *Khamoshi* and *Safar*; Basu Chatterji's *Sara Akash*; Mani Kaul's *Uski Roti*. From the South, I would choose Ramoo Kariat's *Chhemeen* and *Seven Nights*.

You will observe that I have mentioned films from all genres—commercial, experimental, realistic, historical—because, I believe, we need all kinds of films to give a well-rounded picture of a country. *Pather Panchali* is a great film but if some foreigner sees only that and nothing else, he will get a lopsided view of India.

Of course, this is not an exhaustive list; it is merely illustrative, you can add to it or subtract from it. I have merely mentioned some of the films which have made an impact of some significance, and which illuminate some aspect of Indian reality. Today, thanks to the Film Institute, and the Film Finance Corporation, there is a surge of creativity, even in commercial cinema. For instance, I have just seen a film made by Babu Ram Ishara, a young man in his early 20s who wasn't in the Film Institute, who has not even been to college—he was a dialogue writer in commercial films—yet he has directed a daring and poignantly beautiful film called *Chetana*, with completely new artistes, and made it in colour on a shoestring budget. It made a great impression on me.

SK: I notice that you have scrupulously avoided mentioning any of your own films. Is that modesty?

KAA: It is not modesty. But I do believe that one cannot and one should not judge one's own creations. One should leave it to others to evaluate them. You see, I like all my films.

SK: In your opinion, has Indian cinema been able to serve the cause of the common man?

KAA: Each filmmaker claims to be serving the cause of the common man because they all feel that the common man needs and demands entertainment and they are providing it. I remember an incident when Jawaharlal Nehru asked a well-known filmmaker from the South, "Why don't you make films for children?" And his reply was, "Well, Sir, all the films I make are for children." So what it amounts to is that, according to them, the mental age of our cinegoers is not over 13 years.

I believe that people should not only be given what they want but also what they should have. And if we just serve the masses by providing the entertainment they want, and to which they get used to in the course of time, and if this continues, there would come a stage when there will be no scope for artistic expression.

Apart from that, I do feel that in most successful Indian films, there is a certain amount of what I would call the grain of truth—the grain of moral truth and the grain of social truth. I would illustrate it by saying that some of the very crude Indian films which have become very popular were those which were projecting a socially progressive viewpoint, whose sympathies were trained on the side of the underdog, the proletariat or the common man.

I feel that, from this point of view, it is worthwhile to analyse the success of some of the bigger box-office hits, and this analysis should not only be artistic and cinematic but also sociological. I think we will find that, in the collective unconscious or subconscious of our audience, there is a craving for a better life, for a change in our social system, even a justifiable subconscious craving for the good things of life—the material comforts—which perhaps explains the popularity of the films with an opulent atmosphere, amongst the underprivileged masses. And when they get a film with progressive social content, along with the crude entertainment, songs and dances, they accept it more readily than they would accept a film which has a cynical approach to life or which has an anti-progressive approach to social problems. The sentimentality of our people is an axiom which we have to learn to accept.

SK: Mr. Abbas, when you say that the producers provide what the masses demand (and I know many other producers also make the same point) where would you draw the line? What would you say of some of the big-budget films, with all the ingredients of the formula films, failing miserably at the box office?

KAA: Probably they did not have the grain of truth which touched the subconscious urges, strivings and aspirations of the audience. As I have said already, this phenomenon needs to be analysed. Moreover, I should say that there is a repetition of various things. If you make a film with a particular type of dance and song, it may be successful for the first time, but if you make a dozen films of the same type, they would obviously be a failure. The paradox of cinema is that people expect the same kind of entertainment, but at the same time they expect something new. Sometimes, by putting a new set of stars in a film, the same kind of routine formula is given a new look and the audiences accept it more readily.

SK: Your films depict the plight of human beings in a society like India, and you've been concerned a great deal with social problems. What impact do you think your films had on the classes for which you make these films?

KAA: Not very substantial, I am afraid, for the simple reason that my films have to compete with very attractive, very glossy, very colourful films full of dances and songs, with big budgets, popular stars, which are lavishly produced and then released in theatres. So, while competing with such films, my films find it difficult to reach a very wide audience. Moreover, the tastes of the audiences in places where commercial Hindi films have been regularly shown, have been set for a particular type of films. So there is resistance to any other kind of film, that is very difficult to break.

Having said that, I must add that my films do attract a certain class of audience. We have found that my films are appreciated more by the younger lot—students, and young, educated and socially conscious people of the white collar working class. But this is a minority audience sufficient enough to keep the houses full for only a couple of weeks, at most. What is important is that this audience exists and needs to be enlarged, and I am sure with the success of a film like *Bhuvan Shome,* it is not so difficult to build this audience up. Mrinal Sen has opened a new door. Wherever his film has been released, it has attracted a large number of audiences; it is getting crowded houses. Build a chain of art theatres, and you would consolidate and keep on enlarging this minority audience that is growing because of, among other factors, the growth of the Film Society movement.

SK: Finally, what do you think of the idea of censorship? Do you at all think it is necessary, whether in terms of films, literature or the communal situation in various parts of the country?

KAA: I personally think that, ideally, there should be no censorship for creative artists. At the same time, I feel that in a society which is dominated by materialistic values and commercial interests, there should be censorship. These interests being in the hands of socially irresponsible and artistically very crude minds, they can distort every art medium to suit their purpose. Therefore, if there was absolutely no censorship, and the same economic system prevailed, then the unscrupulous commercial interests will exploit this medium by introducing pornography or anti-social themes in a very glossy and technically attractive manner, which may draw crowds of sex-starved cinegoers. Our aesthetic tastes are not so developed and mature to be able to resist this kind of poisonous attraction. If you allow a dancing girl of the crudest type to come and dance on Chowpatty of Bombay or in Delhi at the Ramlila ground at the same time that a politician, a great philosopher, or a great saint is going to make a speech, I am sure the bulk of the audience will turn to the dancing girl. It applies equally to films and, therefore, I would like to have certain regulations on cinema as a medium in the interest of society. For instance, any incitement to communal violence, or religious fanaticism, through the powerful medium of cinema, cannot be allowed and should not be allowed.

At the same time, I would stipulate that censorship should be in the hands of people who are qualified, intelligent, have an artistic approach to cinema, are not conservative or reactionary, who have not got ultra-moralistic tendencies, and they must be dedicated to the ideology to which our country is committed, because I find that some of the films committed to our national ideology run into trouble with the censors.

The latest example of that is my documentary, *A Tale of Four Cities.* This films propagates the socialistic ideology to which our country is, even by the Constitution, committed. But even this documentary, you know, had so much trouble. So, if there are people with reactionary ideas which run counter to our accepted national policies, if they are to judge our films, then the whole purpose of censorship is defeated. For, at the same time, these very censors are allowing, in hundreds of films, the glorification of crime, a very titillating kind of song and dance and scenes which I would call worse than pornography. Nudity is any day preferable to the titillating semi-nudity in some of our films.

SK: How, then, would you sum up the situation in Indian cinema?

KAA: The situation is confusing, contradictory, but not hopeless. I think we are making a breakthrough and, with a little more imaginative encouragement from the government, we can consolidate the hopeful trends in Indian cinema.